Sinners, Survivors and Saints

N.D. Richman

Copyright © 2014 N.D. Richman

First Edition

All rights reserved.

ISBN-13: 978-1496128645
ISBN-10: 1496128648

Edited By:
Gloria Singendonk

Cover Design By:
Bespoke Book Covers

www.NDRichman.com

DEDICATION

For Mom and Dad,
who gave me a childhood I can look back upon with a smile.

ACKNOWLEDGMENTS

Special thanks to:
Marion Chambers
Jane Maxwell
Gary Middleton
Julia Mitchell
Gloria Singendonk

CHAPTER 1

The boat rolled and slammed into the wave trough, splashing salt water over Michael's head. He grabbed the steel tube handhold and stared at the island, the only thing not moving. Michael clenched his jaw. The mansion was buried within the old growth forest, atop the mud brown cliffs. His mom was murdered in that house and Robert Cain, the man responsible, was going to die. Michael just had to find him.

The boat engines roared, pushing Michael, Chris, Thomas, Katherine and their parents further north. A floating pier came into view, protruding seventy feet into the ocean. The captain neared it and swung the boat around, sliding it beside the pier. Two police officers jumped out, grabbed ropes thrown to them by a deck hand, and wrapped them around cleats. "Let's go!" One of them shouted.

"What? We jump?" Jane said.

Michael stepped onto the boat edge, balanced with the pitches, and jumped onto the pier. He turned to Jane and Greg and held his hands up at his sides. "Easy!"

Their parents were huddled together on the pier behind Michael. The boat soared, the mooring ropes snapped taut, and it dropped with a thump, splashing cold seawater over Michael's running shoes. Katherine's eyes went wide. She placed a foot on the boat edge and held out her hand. Michael grabbed it. Her fingers were soft, slender and cold. She hesitated and hopped, landing like a butterfly.

"Thanks, Michael."

"No problem."

Thomas clung to the rail and glared at Michael's outstretched hand. "I'm not a girl," he yelled. Placing his foot on the side he waited for the boat to rise, hopped onto the deck, and staggered over to Katherine.

Chris leapt and appeared suspended in air, like a scene from the Matrix. His over-sized feet walloped the planks and Michael couldn't help but picture a kangaroo.

"Over here," one of the officers called. With dark-brown eyes and a comical grin, he looked like Scooby-Doo at a plate of sandwiches.

Relieved not to be handing out speeding tickets, Michael thought.

To the right of the officer, Thomas and Katherine's mom, Tracy, stood with Michael and Chris's birth parents, Jane and Greg, and adoptive dad, Geoff.

Like Katherine, Tracy had red hair, but her eyes were grey in color, the blue seemingly faded out of them. She clasped her arms around her stomach. Her eyes darted over the waves and she flinched when they crashed onto the rocky shore.

Michael shivered. The September air promised a cold winter.

"Okay, gather around," the officer yelled. "My name is Officer Tim."

Michael leaned over to Chris. "As in donuts."

Chris sniggered.

"Today," Tim said, "we're here to tour the island and gather your statements."

Tim's mustache flopped like a beaver tail when he talked. In spite of his efforts his words were whisked away by the howling wind. Michael leaned forward and cupped his hands around his ears.

"The area is still under investigation. Stay away from the police tape, except for the one at the end of this pier," Tim said. "Chris and Michael, take us to where you landed and lead us through every step, where you stopped, rested, crawled, and especially how you blew up that fuel tank. Leave out nothing."

Michael grabbed his pack and started to walk.

"Uh, could you not bring that?" Tim yelled. "We're supplying lunch."

Michael turned and glared at the officer. "Medication."

Tim's mustache twitched. "Uh, oh, I guess so then."

Michael strode towards the shore. The dock stretched inland like a giant gang plank, meeting a set of stairs that zigzagged to the top of a one hundred foot cliff.

Chris appeared beside him. "Medication?"

A shard of nerves pricked the inside of Michael's stomach. "Shush." He quickened his pace to a near jog. He slowed, ducked under the police tape and ran to the stairs. The stairs were made with wood, long since weathered, and supported with poles jammed into the cliff. They shuddered against the wind gusts. He sighed, dashed up the first flight and paused at the landing. The stairs swayed and he grabbed the railing. Chris, Katherine, and Thomas stood below and stared with their mouths open like dogs catching popcorn.

"No problem," Michael yelled, "they'll hold." He turned and ran, taking the stairs two at a time. Halfway up he stopped and looked over the railing, and imagined the stairs collapsing and driving him into the rocks fifty feet below. It was life threatening and he liked that. He turned and dashed up the next flight.

Michael hopped onto the top deck, leaned over, and panted. The odor of smoke and death was suffocating. Blackened trees littered the ground like discarded matchsticks. A few remained standing, but they clawed from the earth like hands protruding through the mound of a grave. He sat on the splintered wood, hung his legs over the deck, and looked into the ocean. The waves crashed onto shore, creating green troughs that reminded him of his mother's eyes. A lump ballooned in his throat and he swallowed it.

It was weird. He'd dreaded this visit, but now he shivered with anticipation.

Chris and Katherine stepped onto the deck, holding hands. Thomas hopped up behind them.

Katherine scanned the carnage, and the color ran from her face. "It looks like a bomb dropped."

"It did," Michael said.

"So what's the rush?" Chris asked.

Michael stood up and looked down the stairs. Their parents were half way. He looked back at Chris. "Something's wrong."

Katherine frowned and glanced down the stairs. "What?"

"Did you read the news reports? About this? What happened here?"

"Of course," Chris said.

Michael leaned closer. "What's missing?"

Chris and Katherine glanced at each other and stared back at him. "Well?"

"I...I don't know," Chris said.

A wave thundered into the cliff base with a bang, and they jumped.

"Robert Cain," Michael said. "Did you see his name? Anywhere?"

"Nuh, no," Chris said. He looked at Katherine and she shrugged.

"Exactly," Michael said, "never mentioned; they didn't even say this island was his."

"Gee," Katherine said, "I never thought about that. I think you're right."

Thomas stepped from behind Katherine. "But, why?"

"Shush!" Michael said. "They're here."

Tim stepped onto the platform. Michael stepped back to let him pass. He stared at Michael as he walked by. Dad, Jane, Greg, and Tracy followed.

They wound their way up the hillside, single file. Their steps blew clouds of black dust from the ground and Michael's runners turned grey.

"What's with these chunks of metal?" Katherine asked, sidestepping a twisted piece of blackened steel.

"Fuel tank," Michael said.

Tim pointed to a black hunk of shrapnel buried in a tree. "Watch them," he said. "They're sharp."

"How did you guys survive this?" Thomas asked.

"Lucky, I guess," Michael said. He felt an arm around his shoulder and flinched. His dad pulled him in.

"I'm glad," he whispered to Michael.

Michael ducked away.

They reached the top of the hill and the pump house appeared. "Hey! Tim." Michael called.

"Yes, Michael?"

Michael ran to him. "The guy in the pump house, did you find him?"

Tim raised his eyebrows. "Uh, yeah, there was a guy in there. Pretty beat up, how do you know about him?"

"Chris and I, we dragged him in there. He's okay?"

"He survived. You guys put him in the building?"

"Uh-huh."

"You saved his life then. Maybe we should start from this end so we don't have to double back. What happened here?" He pulled out a hand-sized tape recorder and pressed the record button.

Michael walked past him. "Let's start at the fuel tanks." He trudged up the hill and over the crest.

The helicopter lay on its side, charred and rusty like a discarded toaster. The submachine gun no longer swayed on the helicopter blade but lay on the ground.

Thomas stopped. "Whoa!"

"You guys blew up a helicopter?" Katherine asked.

"Yeah," Chris said, "didn't really mean to."

Michael stopped and turned around. Tracy was standing fifteen feet away, her eyes darting over the encircling carnage. She stepped back and stumbled over a tree root.

"Come on!" Michael yelled.

Tracy startled and scurried up the path, glancing behind her as though sensing a stalker.

The group circled around Michael. Tracy pushed through Jane and Greg, into the center of the circle, and folded her arms across her chest.

"There used to be a building, two fuel tanks, and a propane tank by the helicopter," Michael said. "We crept behind one of the tanks. I climbed up and fed a rope into it."

"Where did you get the rope from?" Tim asked.

"Thomas gave it to us back at their farm. It saved Chris's life too, when he fell down a cliff on the mountains."

Thomas smiled and blushed.

Michael walked towards the tanks. Only the metal bottoms were left, and some of the berm remained. He turned around, and they all stood beneath him, bunched together. "A guard heard me open the tank hatch and walked towards us. I jumped on top of him when he came around and Chris hit him on the head."

Chris's chin dimpled. "I thought I'd killed him at first. We dragged him into the pump house."

Michael pointed to the blackened trees below the tank. "I pulled the rope from the tank and dragged it to the trees. We were going to light it and run into the pump house."

Chris walked up beside Michael. "I decided to light the match because Michael was soaked in gas. At first I couldn't get the match to light."

"Then he went up like a Christmas tree," Michael said.

Chris kicked at the ground and dropped his head. His eyes were shut and his jaw trembled.

Chris raised his head and wiped the tears from his cheeks. "I." His voice cracked. "I lit the rope and the air blew up around me. I closed my eyes. I thought they'd been burned out of my skull. I thought I'd never see again. I felt a wave of hot air push down my throat and then I blacked out. I don't remember anything after that, till we saw the house. I could hardly breathe. For the first time ever, Michael could run faster than me." Chris dropped his head and stared at his feet.

Michael put his arm around Chris's shoulder and pulled him in. He could feel Chris sobbing. "Everything went up so fast we didn't get to the pump house. I grabbed Chris and pushed him into the trees." Michael pointed into the tree graveyard. "I threw him on the ground and jumped on top of him as the fuel tank went. Chunks of burning metal flew everywhere and the forest blew into flame. I pulled Chris up and found a path. We stumbled through the forest and up to the house."

They looked at Michael like they were watching a bloody war movie. He smiled. "Questions?"

Tim cleared his throat. "Anyone other than the guard around?"

"Not here," Michael said. "The rest were up by the house. They started to run down after the tank blew, exactly as we'd planned. We blew up the tank to get them out of the house."

"Smart," Tim said, "but stupid. Okay, let's go." He turned and walked towards the camera pole. It wasn't shiny white anymore but grey like a spent charcoal briquette. The camera was missing.

"Hey, Tim!" Michael yelled.

Tim stopped and turned. "Mmm...hmm?"

"The guns, they're still here. When are you gonna collect 'em?"

"Working on it, Michael. We're still gathering evidence from around the house."

They circled the helicopter and marched into the forest. Michael pulled in a deep breath. "Can we go to the beginning, and do the house last?"

"Sure," Tim said, "you can lead us."

Michael's legs throbbed and his stomach growled. They had walked to the cliff and back to the house and it was almost lunch time. The house was black, buckled and riddled with bullets. A sharp pain struck his stomach. He shook with fear and guilt. His mother died in there. Why did she take the bullet? It was meant for him.

"We were standing here when the windows blew," Chris said.

Tim stepped to the house and ran his hand over the mottled siding. "Why?"

"Why what?" Michael asked.

"Why did the windows blow?"

"The propane tank blew up," Chris said. "The whole house leaned back. I thought it was gonna fall over."

Michael picked up a piece of glass about the size of a hunting knife. "We were showered with this stuff."

Chris walked up beside Michael. "Michael jumped on top of me so he took the brunt of it. I pulled three of these things out of his back." Chris's eyes were wet. He looked at Michael and smiled.

Tim pulled a box of rubber gloves from his pack. "We've swept the place, but I need you to wear these, just in case. He passed the gloves around and they pulled them on.

"Proctology convention," Chris whispered as he stepped by. Michael giggled.

Chris crunched through the glass and opened the door. Michael looked back. His dad, Jane, Greg and Tracy had tears running down their cheeks. Parents are so emotional, he thought. He started towards Chris. "Come on. Let's get this over with." He stepped inside and moved forward to make room.

Chris walked to the front and turned to face them like a tour guide. "We were panicking. We knew you guys were in the basement, but we didn't know how to get there."

Chris turned and led them to the kitchen. "I can't remember where we ran or how we found the basement. I think Michael saw it first."

Chris opened the door and looked down the stairs. Michael sidled up beside him and stepped back.

"You don't have to do this, Michael," Jane whispered.

"No, it's okay."

Michael let everyone pass and turned to follow. He stepped onto the checkered tile floor, dropped his head, and bit his lip. He pretended he was a bishop, stepping only on the black tiles and zigzagging from one wall to the other. He imagined a plane of checkered tiles, folded it into a cube, and then shaped it into a donut. He smiled. Shapes comforted him.

He caught up to the rest. They were standing around the desk.

"This is where we found the gun and the keys," Chris said, pointing to the desk.

Michael glanced down a hallway to his right, opposite the one leading to the cells. His heart started to thump. He looked at his dad. "Dad, I don't want to go."

"Okay," his dad replied. "Do you want me to stay with you?"

"No, I'll be fine."

Chris walked around the desk and towards the cells. His dad, Jane, Greg, Tracy, and Tim followed single file. Michael waited until they were twenty feet away and dashed down the hallway to his right. He came to a white door, pulled it open, and stepped inside. He stopped, allowing his eyes to adjust to the dim light. Three sets of quad computer screens sat on a console in the middle of the room. Beyond that, everything faded to black. He placed his hand on the wall behind him and felt his way around the room. The walls were rough. Michael envisioned wallpaper with a vertical candy-stripe pattern.

He could hear their muffled voices. Was someone crying?

His hand struck a doorknob. He grabbed it and pulled the door open. Butterflies invaded his stomach and he clenched his fists. This was stealing, real stealing. And though exciting, it didn't feel right.

He closed the door, brushed the wall with his hand, and found a light switch. He toggled it and banks of fluorescent lights high above fluttered into existence. The room was rectangular, about the size of his bedroom, and painted a stark white. Server cabinets, five black monoliths, formed a Stonehenge like circle in the middle of the room. Server fans whirred like a dentist drill. He dashed to the first cabinet, popped open the door, and scanned the servers.

Chris had discovered Michael's genius last year, but there was still a lot Chris didn't know. Michael's real smarts were computers and programs. Michael guessed there wasn't a twelve year old in the world that programmed like he did.

"Yeah, RAID 5."

There were five hard drives in a RAID 5 configuration. Any two drives held enough information to re-create the entire data set. He zipped open his backpack and pulled a hard drive about the size of a ham sandwich out of the server. He placed it in a cushioned pocket inside the backpack. "Better take three, just in case." He pulled out two more drives and placed them into the backpack beside the first. He zipped the pack up, turned off the light, and left, closing the door behind him.

"Robert Cain, I'm on to you now."

CHAPTER 2

Michael's back hurt. He pushed away from the monitor's glare, stretched, closed his eyes, and listened. His dad, Jane and Greg were downstairs talking over a cup of coffee. The words were muffled, but they sounded serious. Not that there had been much laughter in the house since Mom had died. At least Dad came home from work now. He'd be leaving the house soon to pick up Chris and Katherine at the movies.

It was June. Michael wished his memories had vanished with the snow, but they lay bare like an open wound. A dark vacuum of emotion, sorrow, anger and guilt, grew inside his head. Staying busy was Michael's only means of keeping it at bay, and he had worked at this computer every night for the past six months, scanning the hard drives for information.

A chair scraped over the tiled floor downstairs, jolting him from his daydream. He glanced at the screen. Something caught his eye. Buried amongst the list of files was one that looked familiar. He punched the filename into Google.

"Yes, data vault."

He had to crack it. He started the data vault and stared at the login and password boxes, licking his lips. He clicked an icon, booting up the password cracking software, selected some rules and downloaded the latest wordlist. This wouldn't be easy and might take weeks. Combinations of numbers and letters lit the room like TV snow.

The front door slammed. His dad's truck started up. Michael watched it back out of the garage and accelerate down the driveway.

Michael stared at the numbers and trembled. He shook like this every night.

Robert Cain had to die.

"Michael, do you want to watch a movie?" Jane called.

Michael jumped. "Uh, sure, I'll be right there." He sprang from the seat and padded downstairs.

CHAPTER 3

Michael stepped into the barn and pulled the sliding door closed. He puffed out his chest and smiled while scanning the cathedral-like building. Jane and Greg had it built last fall. Five horse stalls lined the wall to his left. A John Deer tractor was parked in the middle. Four portrait windows were placed along each of the west and east walls. A wooden step ladder, resting on the dirt floor, reached to a balcony. It was a bright and happy place. Jane and Greg offered them the balcony to build as they pleased, and gave them the money to do it.

Sylvester, their cat, dashed from under the tractor and chased a mouse across the barn and into a hay bale. The cat crouched and stared at the bale, ears tweaked forward and tail twitching. Last fall, the cat had popped out of the woods after the barn was built. They adopted him. Sylvester was jet black with golden eyes that looked straight through you. Only Thomas could get near him. He was still a bit wild.

Michael strode to the ladder and climbed up it, walked across the mezzanine and into a room the size of a two car garage. "Hi, Katherine."

"Hi, Michael." She yanked a panel of pink insulation out of a plastic bag and held it away from her like a smelly diaper. Strands of her hair stuck to her forehead and she blew at them. "What do I do with this stuff?"

"Here, let me show you." He hopped over a pile of lumber and sidestepped a stack of drywall. He pulled a mask from a box and placed it over his mouth, and gave a second one to Katherine. "Put this on." Reaching out he grabbed the panel between his thumb and index finger. About four inches thick, it was as wide as his shoulders, about his height, and fluffy and light. He carried it to the wall. "The studs are sixteen inches across and so is the insulation. Place the first piece in like this." He placed the insulation between the wood studs and patted it in. "Make sure it stays fluffy. Don't smush it. When you reach wiring split it in half like this. Put one part behind the wire and the other in front." Michael grabbed the ends of the insulation panel and pulled it in half, making two pieces half as thick. He ran one behind the power wire and one in front. He looked back at Katherine. She looked impressed. "And don't take off those gloves. You'll itch forever."

Katherine placed the mask over her mouth and nose. "It's a pretty color. What's it made of?"

"Glass fibers."

Thomas staggered in with a monster roll of clear plastic on his shoulder. "I've got the plastic."

Michael grabbed a hammer stapler from the floor. "Great, Thomas. Here's the stapler. After the insulation is in we have to staple the plastic over it. Do you know how to use it?"

Thomas threw the plastic roll on top of a piece of wood, catapulting a chunk of drywall across the room and dead into the back of Katherine's head. It blew into a cloud of dust and she dropped to her knees and shrieked. Michael grimaced.

Thomas froze. "Did I do that?"

Katherine turned and glared at him. "I don't know, you little monster. Did you?"

"Uh, sorry?"

Katherine stood and rubbed her head. She scowled. "Geez, I'm gonna have a goose egg now."

Thomas smiled.

He was so eager to please it tired Michael just to watch him. "How'd you get that roll up the ladder, Thomas? It must weigh forty pounds."

"I almost fell."

"Be careful, you little fart. You get hurt and I'll never hear the end of it."

The barn doors squealed. Michael dashed to the mezzanine edge as Chris stepped through with a huge grin on his face. He stopped and looked up at Michael. "How's it going?"

"Excellent. Drywall should be up today. Electrical and computer cables are run. Furnace and air are in, and we have a toilet!"

Chris walked to the ladder. "Wow. You can hardly tell there's a room up there. So when will we be done?"

"Next week. Contractor's taping the walls tomorrow, then, the false floor and server cabinets."

"And the fridge, TV, and stove?" Chris asked.

"Coming next weekend. Dad said he'd help us. The projection TV will be awesome. It covers the entire west wall."

Chris climbed up the ladder. "Greg and I finished the cabinets, table, and chairs. The bookshelf should be ready tomorrow."

Michael led Chris into the room. "Great. Come on then. Lots to do. Oh, by the way, I incorporated our company. It's called MecTek Investigations Inc."

"MecTek?"

"Michael en' Christopher, Thomas en' Katherine."

Chris placed his hands on his hips. "Starting with you, of course."

"Yeah. CemTek didn't have as nice a ring to it. Sounded too industrial."

"How 'bout Search for Robert Inc. or something like that?"

"He won't be our only case. I've already taken one on for our neighbor."

"Which one?"

"Rod. A green van's been prowling around his driveway. He wants us to find out why."

"Cool. Have you started on it?"

"I've ordered a camera. We just have to get power out there."

"Photocells?"

"No, batteries, too many trees. Anyway, let's get moving. We can't solve anything without a place to do it."

CHAPTER 4

The air was sick and humid. It stunk of burnt hair and stung Michael's skin. He breathed in short gasps to dampen the pain.

Sweat trickled down his hair, cheeks, neck, and arms. It dripped off his nose and fingers and crept into the security of his clothes. His shirt, now drenched, surrendered the sweat to his pants. A dark line formed just past his knees.

He stumbled over rocks and into slimy things protruding from the walls. What are those? he wondered, more from curiosity than fear.

It appeared he was encased in a tunnel, but worse, he could sense something ahead. It crouched on the floor of a large cavern and flooded the place with evil. It drew Michael in and seemed to gather satisfaction with each of Michael's steps.

Why? What does it want?

Terror racked Michael. The screams of a million children filled his head. The hair on his arms sprung forward as though attracted to a magnet.

Stop Michael! Stop! Now!

He pushed on.

He tripped, hit the slimy side of the tunnel, recoiled, and fell to the ground. His knees cracked into a rock surface. Pain burst up his legs and into his back like a lightning bolt. He clenched his teeth, trying not to pass out. He wanted to cry, but he was too scared.

A green light appeared from the floor and rose to the ceiling. It glittered against the sarcophagus like walls and they shimmered like a fish tank. Michael sunk to the floor and whimpered.

The light morphed into a glowing mist. The mist swirled into the form of a woman. She floated to the ceiling and looked down at him. Her long dress caressed the floor. Her eyes glowed green, a glittering, innocent green like that of an emerald.

"Michael?" she called.

"Mom?"

"Mom!"

Michael sprinted after her. She receded. He ran harder. She became smaller and smaller. She disappeared.

"MOM!"

Michael threw his fear aside and pushed forward. Seeing only the faint glow of his wristwatch, he ran his right hand over the sweaty wall and stumbled over the mottled floor. He considered that the cave might come to a crushing end on the very next step, tossed the thought aside, dropped his head, and ran.

Light flooded the cave from a hole in the floor. A bridge spanned the hole. Michael surged forward and leapt onto the bridge. It snapped and crumbled under him. He plummeted. His stomach pushed into his lungs. He flailed his arms and legs like a spider grappling for a life saving strand of silk web.

His mother appeared beneath him. Michael stretched his hand out to her, just touching her fingers. She loved him so much.

Red eyes appeared from the cave walls. Teeth tore at his body. His mother started crying. She was fading. She looked so sad, so terrified.

"Mom!"

Michael screamed. He wanted to hit the bottom. He wanted death to snatch him out of the pain. He wanted to join his mother.

Something hard encircled his chest and pinned his arms down. He didn't fight back. It would end soon.

The glow from his mother's eyes swept through his chest, into his arms, down his thighs, through his knees, and into his feet and toes. His body tingled. He grew calm. He was at peace. He fell towards the light.

"I'll protect you," she said.

"Michael! Michael! Wake up!"

"No!"

"It's a dream."

Michael opened his eyes. Chris was on top of him, holding him to the bed.

"I saw her, Chris. I saw Mom."

"No, you didn't. It was a dream."

Michael clenched his fists. "I just about touched her. It wasn't a dream. I saw her."

The bedroom door burst open. Their dad, Jane and Greg rushed in.

"What's going on?" Jane asked.

"Another nightmare," Chris whispered.

"Why did she have to go? Why not me! That bullet was meant for ME!"

Jane sat on the bed, grabbed Michael, and pulled him into her arms. "She does live. She lives in you. She lives in your eyes, your mind, and your soul. She left us so she could live through you."

Michael cried until his head felt heavy. His limbs turned loose. "I killed her," he whispered. The bruises on his knees hurt. He swooned into sleep.

CHAPTER 5

Michael swung away from his computer, stretched, and scanned their new headquarters. The fridge and stove were trimmed with stainless steel. The polished mahogany table and chairs, made by Chris and Greg, glowed under the sodium lights in the kitchen area and a red leather Lazy-Boy couch lay in front of a twelve-foot wide projection TV screen. The computer desks were motorized and could be raised. Sometimes, Michael liked to work when he was standing. Each of them had a large screen iMac tied to a central server. He breathed deep and grinned. The place was perfect.

Katherine was hunched at her computer screen. She was searching for references to Robert Cain, and she looked like she'd found something interesting. Thomas pulled open the oven door and tossed in a frozen pizza. Chris stared sideways into his computer screen while chugging a can of Mug root beer.

"Hey, guys," Michael said.

They turned and looked at him.

"Robert Cain is big in the United Nations. Did you know that?"

"Huh?" Chris clenched his jaw and his forehead creased. "The UN? Why would we care?"

Michael grinned. Chris creased his forehead when annoyed, and he was always annoyed when Michael knew something he didn't; which happened often. "You won't find it in the news, but his name is smeared all over UN documents."

"What does he do at the UN?" Katherine asked.

"Scarcity."

"What's that?" Thomas asked.

"It's freaky," Michael said. "They want to control the world."

"That's silly," Chris said.

Thomas closed the oven door and strolled to Michael. "How?"

"Resources. Control resources, control everything."

"Like what?" Thomas asked.

"Everything," Michael said. "You wanna buy a cell phone, a computer, gasoline for your car, clothes, a bike, food, pretty well everything we use comes from raw resources. They'll control all of it."

Katherine pushed back from her computer. "What kind of resources?"

"All of 'em. Oil, gold, uranium, diamonds, trees, water. As soon as it comes out of the ground, the UN would own it."

"Really? The whole world?" Thomas asked.

"Yep, the whole world."

Chris hopped from his chair and walked to the table, placing his empty root beer can on it.

"In the recycle!" Katherine snapped at him.

Chris glared at her. "You're always telling me what to do." He grabbed the can and whipped it into the bin. "Anyway, how could they do that, Michael?"

"They're almost there," Michael said. "They're building a UN military for enforcement. Robert's heading up the whole thing. He's friends with the US president. Did you know that?"

Katherine's eyes bugged. "Seriously? I didn't find any of this." She turned to her computer and pounded the keys.

The timer buzzed. Chris turned it off, opened the oven, and pulled out the pizza. "Come and get it, guys." Michael and Thomas dashed over and grabbed a plate from the table.

Chris grabbed another root beer and popped it open.

"You're drinking too much of that stuff," Katherine said.

Chris stared at her, over the top of the can, and chugged it down.

"So, Katherine, found anything?" Michael asked. Chris tossed a piece of pizza on to Michael's plate.

Katherine turned to face him. "I don't know what to say, Michael. Most of these are conspiracy sites. They're kind of creepy. There's no real proof he's friends with the president."

"The president can hide anything. Right?"

"I'm sure the media... "

"Ha!" Michael blurted. "The media? The truth? Serious?"

Katherine turned back to her screen. "Well, maybe. Anyway, he is involved in the UN, like you said. And he's leading a committee. It was struck by the commission for social development."

"Yeah, and what's that committee up to?"

Chris snuck by Michael and sat at his computer.

Katherine pursed her lips. "Just like you said."

Michael sat in his chair and wheeled up beside Katherine. "And they have a lot of countries on board?"

"India, all of Africa, the EU, Russia, and most of Asia. Hmmm...almost all the middle east countries. Strange, why would they give up their oil? But not the US, and they'll need the US to pull off something this big."

Michael jumped from his chair. "Asia? As in China?"

"Yep, but not Japan."

"Wow, that's new. They've got most of the globe locked in. How 'bout South America?"

"All but Brazil and Chile. As far as North America, Mexico signed up but not Canada or the US."

Thomas walked over and sat down beside Katherine. "But how will they force countries to hand over their resources?"

Katherine scanned her computer screen. "Those signed up agree to buy resources only from the UN, and they're making a global law so it'll be illegal for corporations to buy or sell resources through anyone but the UN. Once the UN has a lock on buyers, producing countries will be forced to sell to the UN for cash. They've already started the process in the EU," Katherine said. She swung back to her screen. "Anyway, I can't find new references to Robert Cain, but the committee is still working."

"Hey, Michael," Chris called.

"What?"

"Do you remember that e-mail from Greg, about the machine at the lab?"

"Uh-huh."

"The lab made an application to the government to install a 70 megawatt turbine on the site."

"Is that a big one?" Thomas asked.

"Enough to power the whole city," Michael said.

Katherine hopped off her chair. "A machine? What machine?"

Chris swallowed his pizza. "Greg and Dad were e-mailing about some kind of machine. They were really excited 'cause it zapped a fruit fly, or something."

"A seventy megawatt bug zapper?" Thomas asked.

They all laughed.

"Dunno," Michael said, "but they're up to something."

Chris swiveled his chair around. "Michael, Dad mentioned something to me just after Mom died."

"What?"

"About a machine. He wouldn't tell me what it was, but Robert wants it real bad."

"The same one in the e-mail?"

"Pretty sure. He said it was at the lab. He and Mom were working on it."

Michael felt his ears turn red. "So the whole story about us isn't true?"

"No, all true, Michael. Jane and Greg are our birth parents, and her brother does want us dead to save his fortune. It's just that this machine is involved too. Robert was looking for it, and that's how he found the link, between Jane and Greg and Mom and Dad."

"Nice of Dad to share it with me." Michael glared at Chris. "Did you find out anything else about the lab?"

"Nope. The place is a rock-solid secret. I found a reference to military weapons. They work for the American and Canadian departments of defense."

"It's gotta be a weapon."

"Yeah, destroying fruit flies throughout the world," Thomas said. He giggled.

Michael laughed. His computer beeped. He looked at the screen and smiled. Sitting down, he punched in a password. His hands tingled. A web site sprung from the screen like a shower of diamonds.

He jumped up and threw his arms in the air. "Yes! I've got it!"

Chris jerked back, knocking his root beer into his lap.

"Geez, Michael. Got what?" Chris brushed the pop out of his crotch.

"His bank account."

"Really?" Katherine and Thomas said in unison.

Chris, Thomas, and Katherine dashed to Michael's chair. He flinched. "Whoa, guys!"

Thomas popped up in front.

"I've been trying to crack a program on Robert's computer for weeks," Michael said. "I got in last night. It's a data vault used to store passwords and login IDs. Now, for the important part." He pointed at the monitor. "Look at this here."

"Richman?" Katherine said. She pulled her lips into a pout. "What the heck does Richman mean?"

"Look above, over here, Bronds Bank."

"Come on, Michael. You're killing me. Just spit it out," Chris snapped.

"This is a Cayman Islands bank. The minimum account balance is one hundred thousand. Now, look at this number here, 111557934752-23. This is a bank account number."

"You have Robert's account, with all his money?" Chris asked.

"Yep, but not all his money. There's four more accounts."

"How much?" Thomas asked. His voice squeaked.

"Money? I need a password for that."

Chris groaned. "What is it?"

Michael called up a third display.

"What's that?" Chris asked.

"Login. I entered Robert's user ID, RichMan23. He's a little brash, eh? Any guesses on the password?"

"I'm not guessing!" Chris yelled.

"I'm not going to tell you then," Michael taunted.

"Doh! I'm gonna... "

Michael felt Chris's cold fingers wrap around his throat.

"Chris-to-pher!" Katherine screeched. "Get your hands off him!"

Chris dropped his hands. "Can't I strangle him just a bit?"

"No, he's your brother!"

"What's your point?"

Katherine punched Chris on the shoulder.

Michael grinned.

"I'll give you a hint. Robert changed it the day we invaded his island."

"Boom?" Thomas said.

They laughed.

"What was it, Michael?" Chris asked.

"Hold on. His phone number and credit card number are listed as well. And look at this." Michael scrolled down. "There are four names, each with credit card and bank account numbers."

Katherine put her hand on Michael's shoulder and leaned forward. "Joe Vinte, Geoff Sander, Jim Ponto, Dave Gant. Who are they, Michael?"

"Robert Cain."

"Huh?"

"Robert Cain created four more names for himself. No wonder we can't find him. He's using a different name."

"Which one?" Thomas asked.

"This account is listed under Joe Vinte."

"And the password?"

"LittleBratz."

"LittleBratz?" Chris said.

"I figure we were really ticking him off. Not a very secure password. Anyway, here goes."

"L-i-t-t-l-e-B-r-a-t-z-2-3." Michael said as he typed.

Katherine leaned over Thomas. "Why the 2-3?"

"Just a hunch. The last two digits of the account number."

Michael hit enter. The display paused. The computer beeped. Words popped up.

Welcome Mr. Vinte. Would you like to view your account?

"Yahoo!" Chris jumped and clapped. Katherine shrieked. Thomas danced like a bobble head on the dash of a pickup truck. Michael leaned back, puffed out his chest, and grinned.

Michael moved the cursor and clicked the 'Yes' target.

The computer fan's indiscernible buzz flooded the vacuum of silence. The wall clock ticked three times. Thomas gasped.

"Seventy nine million, six hundred and twenty five thousand, four hundred and thirty two dollars and eleven cents," Chris whispered. "If only it was mine."

Michael looked at him. Chris was a little grey.

"It is yours," Michael said. "Remember? The entire estate is yours on your next birthday."

"Yeah, but no one knows this exists."

"We do," Michael said. "Here." He turned around and popped open another explorer window and typed in a TCP/IP number. A website popped up. "This is an alternative payment channel. I set it up a few months ago."

"A what?" Thomas asked.

"It's a way to transfer money."

"Is it legal?" Katherine asked.

Michael turned and looked at her. "This one? Not really. Took a bit to set it up."

Katherine's face flushed, matching her hair. "How can you possibly know all this stuff?" she asked.

"Boy genius," Michael said. "No one told you?"

Chris folded his eyebrows and glared. "Yeah, genius when doing stuff you shouldn't."

"True," Michael said. "Anyway, I just logged in. Watch this."

Michael selected a 'Transfer' target in the alternative channel. He entered $79, 625, 432.10 in the amount box followed by a 14 digit number in the account box, and hit enter.

"Here, look at Robert's account now," Michael said.

"One cent?" Katherine whispered. "He'll know. He'll know someone did this to him."

"Yep, ain't it fun?" Michael said.

Michael felt someone lean onto his back. "Where did it go?" Chris whispered.

Michael swung his chair around and grinned. Chris's skin was opaque. "I set up some automatic transactions. Gold, silver, oil, diamonds, titanium, and pork bellies."

Chris's mouth dropped. "Huh?"

"We just bought a bunch of stuff. Expensive metals was an easy choice. Pork bellies, I just like bacon. In five minutes it'll be sold and the proceeds placed in an offshore account I set up for us. Then, the trading accounts will vanish from the world."

Chris licked his lips. "Seriously?"

"Yep, we're officially stupidly rich."

Katherine leaned back and placed her hand on the table beside her. "Chris? Will you marry me?"

Chris flushed like a fire truck.

"Gold digger," Michael said.

Katherine smacked him on his head. Michael ducked and poked her belly button.

"You little rat," she said. "You can't touch me like that."

Michael swung back to the computer screen. "Dish it, take it.

Anyway, I'm gonna pay off Robert's credit card with this empty bank account. They'll flag his card and he won't be able to use it."

"Won't that tick him off?" Thomas asked.

"Yeah, probably." Michael entered the credit card number and password into the website, and clicked enter.

"I don't know, Michael. Won't he figure out who has his money?" Katherine asked.

"No, he can't track it."

The account popped up. Michael selected the pay-all option and pressed enter. He swung around.

Thomas's eyes darted between Michael and Katherine. "But, one cent? Who would leave just one cent?" Thomas asked.

"There's no way he'll guess it was us," Chris said.

Katherine glanced at Michael. Her dimples deepened. "Who the heck else would it be? He might go after us."

"Naa," Chris said, "he'll just move on to his next name. Seventy-nine million is nothing to this guy."

"I tried the other accounts, but the passwords don't work," Michael said.

Chris bounced on his toes. "Yay! We're rich!"

"Can we buy a Lamborghini?" Thomas asked.

"Sure, Thomas," Michael said. "We can buy one for each of us."

"Michael," Katherine blurted. "I think I saw a bank letter addressed to Geoff Sander. I was reading a bunch of scanned documents from Robert's server."

"Start looking then. Geoff Sander's the next name on the list. He'll probably go for that one. Thomas and Chris, try to find Robert, uh Joe Vinte, before he changes his name to Geoff Sander. Katherine, you look for that letter."

CHAPTER 6

"I'll beat ya!" Michael yelled as he dashed out of their room. It was the first day of summer. The smell of bacon and eggs filled the house. Dad was cooking breakfast again.

Michael hopped onto the stool at the island and grabbed a glass of orange juice. Chris shuffled in and plopped down beside him.

"Rough night, Chris?" his dad asked.

"I need a cup of coffee," Chris said.

"It'll stunt your growth."

Michael looked at his dad and grinned. "And that's a bad thing?"

His dad smiled. "One egg, or two?"

"Two please," Michael and Chris answered in unison.

Michael popped the egg yolks and watched the liquid gold spill into the hash browns. He mixed it up, grabbed a piece of bacon and pushed it into his mouth sideways. He crunched the greasy goodness and shoveled some potatoes into his mouth. No one made a better breakfast than his dad. He swept up the last bit of egg on the plate with his toast, chewed it down, and hopped off the stool. "Thanks, Dad."

"Hold on, Michael," his dad said. "We want to talk to you." Glancing at Chris, Dad nodded his head to the side indicating Chris should leave the room.

"See you later," Chris said. He hopped off the stool and dashed to the front door.

"Come with me, Michael."

Michael followed his dad to the library. Jane and Greg were already there, sitting on the sofa. Michael's heart beat faster and his palms grew sweaty. He was in trouble, but worse, he didn't know why.

His dad closed the door. "Sit down, son."

Michael slid into the leather chair and the cushion wheezed. He didn't laugh.

Jane looked at her feet, and she was rubbing her toes together. Greg was sitting on his hands. His mouth formed a tight line.

Michael's dad sat beside Jane. "Michael, how are you feeling?"

Michael's temples tightened. He glanced at the floor. The rug had little lady bugs weaved into it. Funny, he'd never noticed that before. "Fine."

"We've noticed you've been moody lately, and the dreams."

"Uh-huh."

What are they up to? They're not going to send me away, are they?

"Michael," Jane said.

Just spit it out.

"Your mother's death has been hard on all of us but mostly on you. We think you need help dealing with it."

Numbness spread from Michael's fingers and through his arms. He clenched his fists.

No.

"We've found someone we think can help," his dad added. "He specializes in this type of thing."

"What thing?" Michael asked.

"Just someone you can talk to," Jane said.

Michael clenched his fists and jumped from the chair. "I'd rather die! I'm not crazy!"

"Michael." His dad rushed over and put his arm around Michael's shoulders. Michael recoiled and shoved his dad, knocking him to the floor. He ran through the door and down the hall. He glared at Bill's face peering through the front door window. "Ghosts are everywhere," he muttered. "Go away!" He charged out of the house and into the front yard.

"Michael!" his dad yelled.

The lawn sunk under Michael's feet. He sprinted across the yard and to the riverbank. He vanished into the white stand of birch trees, turned and ran west alongside the river. The tall grass tore at his knees and tears blurred his vision. He cried out loud and he hated nothing more than crying. "I'm not crazy!"

He burst into a circled space and ran to his mom's headstone, placed in the centre and surrounded with a pile of fresh flowers. He fell to the grass. His knees sunk into it.

"Why you, Mom? Why you? I thought you didn't care. I thought you didn't like me. And that bullet was for me!"

A flock of nightingales burst from the tree tops and streaked away. The leaves rustled. The trunks swayed and groaned. The sky turned black. Lightning streaked. Fat rain drops drove into his back.

He pressed his face into the wet grass, closed his eyes, and sobbed.

CHAPTER 7

"Hello?"

"Hello, sir. Could you please come to the lobby? We're having a problem with your credit card."

Robert Cain grunted. He placed his wine glass on the hot tub edge and whipped a towel off the rack.

The towel struck the glass and knocked it into the tub. A blood river swirled through the water and bubbled to the surface like molten lava.

"Crikey!" He hit the off button and pulled the plug. "I was just starting to relax." He pulled his muscular form from the tub, toweled dry, and pulled on a T-shirt and a pair of shorts.

"A trillionaire, and they're worried about my stupid credit card," he muttered while pulling open his hotel room door.

He walked into the cathedral hallway and grinned. "A run before breakfast, work out in the morning, firing range an hour a day, a drive in my Ferrari, dealing with those idiots at the UN, and a glass of wine every night. What could be better than this?"

Robert admired the angels painted on the ceiling as he approached the elevator. He punched a crystal button and waited. The elevator appeared in seconds and whisked him to the lobby.

The hotel manager, a roly-poly man with Harry Potter glasses, stood at the elevator doors.

"Hello, Mr. Vinte. Could you please come to my office?"

Robert rolled right into his alias. "You can call me Joe, Jim. How many times do I have to tell you that? Nothing serious, I hope."

"No, Mr. Vinte, I'm sure we can get it resolved."

Jim led Robert to his office. It was cavernous, with walls and floors of polished marble. A black iron chandelier, five feet in width, hung from the ceiling on a ten-foot chain. Jim sat at a maple desk, as large as a queen sized bed, centered under the chandelier.

"Please have a seat, Mr. Vinte."

"Great. Thanks."

Jim's tongue darted like a gecko smelling the air for signs of danger.

Robert walked over a plush Persian rug and sat across from Joe in a burgundy leather chair.

"There seems to be a problem with your credit card, Mr. Vinte. Your last month's bill wouldn't go through. We talked to your card company. Apparently, there's an issue with your funds."

"Can I borrow your computer? I want to check my account," Robert said.

"Yes, please, go ahead."

A computer monitor and keyboard sat on the desk, facing Robert. He logged onto the internet, accessed the Bronds Bank web site, and typed in his account number - 111557934752-23.

"Little brats," he mumbled while typing in the password.

"Pardon?"

"Oh, nothing."

Robert's skin prickled. Warmth flooded his limbs and pooled in his feet. He felt sick.

"Are you all right, Mr. Vinte?"

"Guh."

Jim stood from his chair. "Can I help you?"

"Guh, one cent?"

"Can I help you, Mr. Vinte?"

"No! Leave the room!"

"Uh, sure. No problem, Mr. Vinte" Jim jumped up and scurried from his office.

Robert screamed and pounded his fist on the desk. He logged into the Geoff Sander account.

"300 million," he whispered.

"Jim Ponto, 500 million.

"Let's see. Dave Gant, 600 million."

He logged off and stomped out of the office.

"You'll have your money in the morning," he snapped.

Robert stormed onto the elevator and stabbed the button with the ferocity of a child whacking an arcade mole. "Those freakin' kids. It's gotta be those kids. But how could it be? No way." He kicked the stainless steel elevator wall. "Not possible!"

"I'll kill 'em. I'll tear them apart. Brats. Little brats." He cracked his knuckles.

"Really though. How could they?"

The elevator doors opened and he stomped down the hall. A white light burst through the crack under his door. He raised his arm to shield his eyes and squinted.

"What? What the heck is that?"

Robert started to wheeze. His heart pounded. Hands shaking, he grasped the card key and pulled it from his pocket. He shoved it into the slot. The green L.E.D. in the lock flashed. He grabbed the levered handle and cracked the door open.

The light vanished.

He peeked around as though expecting to be shot.

He took one step in and paused.

"Hello? Is anybody there?"

The room was black. He heard a woman's voice. She was whispering. Or was she crying? Robert couldn't make out what she said, but she scared him to his core. Body warmth fled to his organs and his hands turned cold. He swallowed and stepped in.

"Gah!"

A ball of green light, the size of a mouse, floated from the bathroom door. It dropped a foot from the floor and hovered like a tiger sizing up its prey.

Warmth spread through his shorts. He heard his urine dripping onto the floor. He wanted to look down, but his eyes were pinned.

His knees buckled and he leaned against the wall to arrest his fall.

"What?"

It streaked right at him.

Robert dropped to the floor, curled up, and wrapped his head under his arms. The light shot over him and into the hallway. He looked back as it disappeared through the far wall.

The tile felt cool on his cheek. He could smell urine and Pine Sol. He lay shaking.

"The safe!" He jumped up and dashed down the hall and into the living room. Behind the suede sofa was a gargantuan painting of a unicorn with a lady sitting on it. He grabbed the gold picture frame, swung it open to the safe behind, and pulled on the handle.

"Whew, still locked."

He spun the dial – "right, left, right, right again."

He heard a satisfying click, turned the handle and popped open the safe. He pulled out the papers and sighed.

He counted the one hundred dollar bills with shaking hands. There were nine hundred of them. Gonna need that, he thought.

He sat at his computer, modified his passwords and wrote down the new ones. He placed the notes in the safe and locked it.

He staggered to the bathroom and stared into the mirror. His eyeballs were pink and his skin green. He dropped to the toilet and spewed his dinner, a mixture of blood red wine and digested shrimp.

He sunk to the floor and shook like a paint mixer. *What was that light?*

He grabbed the sink and pulled himself up. Turning on the hot water, he lathered his hands with the hotel soap. It was green, shaped like a seashell, and smelled like flowers and vomit. He pulled off his clothes, slunk into the shower, turned up the hot water till it stung, and then lathered down.

He dried himself, walked from the bathroom and slid into bed. He pulled the covers over his head and fell into a troubled sleep.

Robert opened his eyes. The down comforter lay flat on his face. It was warm and dark. He shivered.

She was out there. He could feel her. He could hear her whispering from deep within his head. "You touch them Robert and you're mine."

Don't be silly, he thought, you're acting like a child.

He closed his eyes, grasped the comforter and lowered it. Crisp, conditioned air stroked his face.

"Open your eyes. Open your eyes." He opened them, and she was there. "Claire?"

She floated at the ceiling. Her dress billowed like a flag in a windstorm. Her emerald eyes pushed terror into his soul. He curled his toes till his toenails scraped the bottoms of his feet.

She started to spin. He surrendered his breath with an imperceptible hiss. Her face turned blue. She swooped down onto him like a burst of cold rain from a thundercloud and passed through his body and into the mattress.

"Agghhhhh!" Robert's legs shook. His teeth chattered. His flesh turned to mush.

"Get up! Get up!" he screamed and threw off the comforter. The cold air hit his sweaty skin with a bite. He slid to the floor, crawled to his cell phone, and punched a phone number into the keypad.

"Hello?"

Robert sat up and leaned against the wall. "Pete?"

"What's wrong?" Pete asked.

"Nuh, nothing."

"It's three in the morning."

"I know!" Robert took a deep breath and shuddered. He placed his hand over his eyes. "How's the house, Pete? Did you find one?"

"Yeah. A big ranch, about 200 acres. It's got a garage, barn, exercise room, swimming pool, and a guest house."

"I need the guest house sealed like a jail cell. Oh, and does it have a landing strip?"

"Yep. Can land the jet there no problem."

"Did you hire someone to manage the place?"

"Yes. Do you want kitchen staff?"

"Uh-huh. And find a security company. A loyal one."

"I've been checking into mercenaries. They're loyal to money."

"Good idea. And the place needs video surveillance."

"Of course. Got it. What's the matter, Robert...uh Joe?"

"The brats stole my money, Pete. I...I'm seeing things."

"Seeing things?"

"Yeah. I...I can't explain. We're going after them. I'm tired of waiting. I want my money back and I want them dead."

"Which ones?"

"All of them."

"Sounds like fun, Joe."

"I'm Geoff Sanders now."

"Great. Okay, Geoff. We'll wait till after you get the machine?"

"No, I want it done now."

"Isn't that taking on a lot?"

"The machine's taken care of. I've got an army lined up for that. I just have to figure out where it is. It's your job to get the kids. Chris and Michael are just as important. I can hide money but if they take my cash flow I'm screwed. The will's with a judge now. I've paid him to slow the process down, but only for a year. If we don't eliminate the kids we'll have to kill the judge and start over."

CHAPTER 8

Michael crunched into a piece of pizza. Hot pineapple juice exploded onto his tongue. "Ow. Tastes great, Thomas."

Thomas sat to his right. Chris was in front of him across the table and Katherine to his left. Chris reached over and grabbed Katherine's hand.

Katherine hit the table with her fist. "Jeez, Chris! You don't have to touch me all the time."

Chris's mouth opened and closed. His forehead creased. "But... "

"But, nothing, sometimes I need MY space. OK?"

Michael stared into the tabletop. He'd felt a tension between Chris and Katherine over the past few months. It was strange. They were usually like polar ends of a magnet.

"Are you guys okay?" Thomas asked.

"We're fine," Katherine snapped.

Michael pushed Chris and Katherine out of his head. His stomach twitched. He jammed his index fingernail between his teeth and bit it off. Becoming a multi-millionaire was a nice touch to his week but the risks bothered him. Like a pebble embedded in the soul of his shoe, something felt out of place. He hadn't slept all week. He saw Bill peeking through the front door window every time he came down the staircase. It was becoming real again, too real. His dad hadn't mentioned the psych ward though, which was one good part of the week. "So? Did you guys find anything this week?"

"The letter was nothing," Katherine said. "The bank offered him a diamond necklace for opening an account with them."

Michael choked on his pizza. "Gee, I didn't get anything for opening ours."

"Maybe they're sending you a Lamborghini," Thomas said. "I searched the internet for Joe Vinte. Found nothing. I also checked those files, Michael, couldn't find a thing."

"Thanks, Thomas," Michael said. "On another note, after Chris installed the batteries, I set up the camera in the neighbor's driveway. We caught something a couple of days ago at eleven in the morning."

Michael grabbed the remote and clicked on the projector. The neighbor's driveway displayed onto the west wall. Michael pressed play. The camera viewed down and along the side of the driveway and centered on a large pile of leaves. A brown squirrel with a bushy tail appeared from under the leaves, dashed to the camera, and sniffed at it. Magnified by the lens, his nut brown nose and white whiskers filled the entire twelve-foot screen.

"Agghhhhh! The squirrel that ate New York!" Thomas yelled. He threw his arms up and fell to the floor screaming.

They burst into laughter.

"Looks like a fairly dangerous squirrel, Michael. I can see why the neighbors are worried. Does it drive?" Chris said.

"Funny," Michael said. He bit into his pizza.

"He's so cute," Katherine said.

The squirrel's tail shot up. The squirrel turned around, hesitated, and darted into the leaf pile.

They heard a motor and tires over gravel. A green van turned into the driveway. It pulled to the side, plowed through the pile of leaves with a whoosh, and stopped. The breaks squealed.

Katherine jumped from her chair "No! They killed him!"

The squirrel, followed by a second one, dashed out of the leaves and leapt over the camera, flashing their white underbellies. Katherine jumped and clapped.

Only the bottom of the van was visible.

Michael paused the video.

"That's it?" Chris said.

"'Fraid so." Michael sauntered to the screen. "He parked for an hour." Goodyear tires, eighty percent worn. It's a three quarter ton Dodge van. One of the pistons isn't firing properly. Needs spark plugs. And there's a knock from a rocker arm."

"You can tell all that?" Thomas asked.

"Yep." Michael pointed to some black spots on the green paint. "These look fresh and they're big, which means the van didn't come from town. They're paving the road to the west. No one left the van that I could see. I moved the camera and added a second one, pointing down from a tree. I should be able to see the license plate next time."

"What can you do with the plate?" Thomas asked.

"Find out who registered the vehicle."

Chris grabbed another piece of pizza. "You can get into the vehicle registration database?"

"Why? That would surprise you?"

Chris sighed. "It's a government database. More stuff I don't want to know?"

"It's a weird place to park," Katherine said. "It's like they're watching someone. I wonder what they're up to?"

Michael picked up his Coke and chugged it down. "No idea. Should find out next time though."

"Not a great week," Thomas said.

"Don't worry, Thomas. We'll find Robert soon. I'm sure of it," Chris said.

"That would be Joe," Michael said.

"Right, Michael, I'm starting to lose track."

"Actually," Thomas said, "he's probably Geoff now."

CHAPTER 9

Katherine pulled away the seventies-orange curtain and gazed into their backyard. The grass was yellow. It looked like it wanted to die. She pulled off her church dress and slipped on a pair of jeans and a crisp white T-shirt. She slung the comforter over her bed and turned to the mirror. She folded her arms and sighed. She pulled the elastic out of her ponytail, shook her head, and let her hair fall onto her shoulders. She loved being a ginger. It was cool, and made her eyes bluer. She had never thought of herself as pretty until she met Chris. He was kind of right. She smiled and enjoyed the dimples in her cheeks.

What should she do? She liked Chris so much it hurt, and she couldn't get him out of her mind. She thought back to the first time she saw him, and smiled. Chris had flown off the balcony in red underwear like a drunken superman. He'd gawked at her like a child ogling an ice cream cone. Chris had been so clumsy and unsure of himself back then. It seemed they had switched places since.

She had wanted to be a doctor when she grew up. Her life had been planned, constant, and predictable. Then Chris came into the picture and messed it all up. She blushed as she recalled their first kiss on that rock in the mountains. Her heart had pounded for days.

Her scalp prickled and she pursed her lips. Chris was smothering her. She needed to be herself again. She needed to think about her future. She wanted to be a doctor, not Chris's sidekick.

She pouted into the mirror. "So, Katherine, what to do? Break up with him?"

She'd been thinking about it for the past month. Saying it was easier than she'd expected. Chris would be really hurt. But what was more important, him or her? Her stomach fluttered and hurt.

"Yep, I'll tell him today." She frowned, stepped out of her room, and bounded up the stairs.

Her mom stood in the kitchen holding a cup of coffee. She was biting the inside of her lip.

Katherine paused at the top of the stairs. "What, Mom?"

"Where are you headed today?"

"I'm going to Chris's. We haven't taken the horses out for a ride since last weekend. We found this beautiful trail along the riverbank. We're gonna check it out."

"Oh." The letter V appeared in the wrinkles on her forehead, just above her nose. She set her cup on the counter. "I'm taking Thomas to get a badminton racket. He can't keep playing with that broken one."

"Yeah," Katherine said, "I think he would've won the tournament last week with a proper racquet. He's a pretty good little player."

Her mom looked at the floor and Katherine regretted the comment.

Her mom looked back up. "Chris's dad invited us over for dinner tonight. How 'bout I just meet you there then."

"Okay."

"Katherine?"

"Uh-huh?"

"You've been spending a lot of time with Chris. Shouldn't you lay off a bit?"

"No, I'm not, Mom. Anyway, It's none of your business."

"Katherine! Don't talk to me like that. I'm worried about your safety. That Robert character might come back. I don't want you caught up in it. Anyway, it wouldn't hurt you to spend some time with your other friends. Remember them?"

"I can take care of myself, Mom. And I'll remember my other friends when I want. And you? Worried about my safety? That's a joke!"

Katherine turned towards the back door. Her mom gasped. Katherine flinched.

"How dare you!" Her mom screamed.

"Whatever!" Katherine yelled back. She stormed down the stairs and charged out the back door. She ran to the garage and unclenched her fists. Her bike, old, scratched, and faded, stood against the west wall. A friend of her mom's had picked it up at a police auction. On Katherine's eleventh birthday her mom had covered her eyes and led her to the garage. She'd jumped up and screamed when she saw it. Although a little rusty and worn, it was a Kuma mountain bike. Brand new, it would have cost thousands. She'd spent the next two weekends tearing it down, cleaning and oiling it, and adjusting the brakes and changer. Last week she replaced the tires and grips. It was a sturdy old friend.

She zipped out of the garage into the heat of the midday sun and rocketed down the alley. It would take an hour to get to Chris's house. She wasn't anxious to get there, but the ride would be fun. She checked for cars and turned south onto the highway. She had a lump in her throat. She felt horrible. With each turn of the pedals, the thought of breaking up with Chris became harder. They had been through so much together. She wiped the tears from her eyes and pushed on.

Katherine leaned her bike into the turn. The back tire popped over a gravel patch, almost slamming her onto the road. She smiled, confident the treads would recover, and careened around the sharp corner, leaving the highway for a paved lane. Pine trees crowded the narrow road but offered little defense against the midday sun. Sweat trickled down the back of her neck.

She stood on the pedals and pumped harder. She grinned, thinking about the news she had. Last night, she'd jumped out of bed in excitement when the thought had come to her. Robert Cain was easy to track. She couldn't believe Michael had missed it.

The front tire spun over the pavement, pulling melted tar off the road and flicking it into the air. Listening to the harmonic buzz, she slipped into another place. She thought of Chris and got a lump in her throat. She wanted to cry. He'd be really upset after all they'd been through together. "Ah well," she sighed. "Go with it."

Something wasn't right. She glanced at the sun and then into the forest. The trees were quiet.

Where's Thomas? Oh, right, with Mom.

She heard a vehicle behind her, accelerating. She snuggled to the shoulder.

A green cargo van with blackened windows pulled up beside her. She smacked it with her hand and yelled, "Move over!"

Something hit her, snapping her head forward and pushing her helmet over her eyes. The van swerved and smashed into her bike. The handle bars popped from her hands. The front tire swung around and smacked her knee, bringing the bike to a crushing stop.

"Agghhh!" She flew over the handle bars. Her helmet hit the gravel, her body flipped over, and she came down on her back.

"Goh!" Her lungs clamped in spasms. She couldn't breathe.

She heard the van screech. Two men jumped out and ran towards her. Dark spots swarmed her brain like flies over a piece of bad meat. She reached into her pocket, pulled out her cell phone, and started to feel out a text.

"Get it!" One of the men yelled.

The phone was wrenched from her hand. Fingers dug into her left bicep. Someone grabbed her right arm. She was pulled into a standing position.

"What do you want from me?" She screamed.

"Shut-up!" Her captor yelled. A fist filled her vision. Her neck snapped back. Pain fired through her jaw. Numbness filled her head. All went black.

CHAPTER 10

Michael launched his new software and leaned back from the computer. Green, purple, and pink patterns exploded over the computer screen, scrolling from the top to the bottom. Chris walked up behind him. "What's with the weird patterns?"

"Does it mean anything to you?" Michael asked.

"Nope."

"Means lots to me. Chris, if you had a whole bunch of information in front of you, and wanted to figure it out, what would you do with it?"

Chris shrugged. "Dunno. Sort it?"

"Exactly. You'd sort it. Reduce it. Make it smaller. I'm different."

Chris grabbed his chair, wheeled it over, and sat beside Michael. "Different? How?"

"I can see patterns in data, especially in lots of data. And even better, I can see patterns in what's missing, as well as what's there. This may look like northern lights to you, but to me its information."

Chris leaned forward and stared into the screen. "Really?"

"Uh-huh. I've been writing a new kind of software. This is the first time I've used it. Only I can understand it. It's searching for information on Robert."

"Searching where?"

"Every server connected to the Internet, and even a bunch not connected."

"Not connected?"

"Not directly."

"Wow," Chris said. "Scary."

"Yeah," Michael said. "It is a little scary. Makes me feel powerful, too powerful sometimes. Anyway, I still gotta write software to capture the important stuff. I can't stare at this screen all day. So, did you find anything?"

Chris leaned back and stretched. "Nope."

"Where's Katherine?"

"She said 2 o'clock. Should be anytime now."

"Is Thomas coming?"

"Not till later. He's with his mom. They'll all be here at four, for dinner."

Chris's cell phone rang out "Makin' this Boy Go Crazy," by Dylan Scott.

He pulled the phone from his pocket and stared into the screen. "Katherine, maybe she can't make it."

Chris's mouth dropped.

"What's the matter?"

"I don't get it, Michael, look."

Michael walked over and peered into the display.

Crdtcrd Hlpme.

"Credit card?"

"Help me?

"What the heck, Chris. Is she held captive by a shopping spree?"

"Not funny. Something's wrong."

"Maybe weird but I don't think wrong. Is she trying to be funny? Think credit card. Maybe she's found a wedding dress?"

Chris glared at him and stood up. "Don't be a jerk. Come on. Let's get our bikes and meet her."

Michael grabbed his bike from the ground and hopped on. He'd built the bike from a frame he'd found at the dump and parts he'd stolen from a scrap yard. It was hand painted green, with black handlebars, a brown seat and eighteen gears. Michael called it FrankenBike.

Chris had already zipped through the barn doors. Michael geared down and pumped hard, and pulled up beside him. They rocketed down the driveway, broke into the forest, and bounced around the gate.

Chris flew onto the road. Michael was a foot behind him. They blew by Rod's driveway.

Michael geared up and sped past Chris. He looked back and yelled, "Ha!" The warm breeze pushed his hair back and dried the sweat on his forehead.

He choked his breaks and skidded to a stop. Chris rammed him, and they crashed to the pavement in a tangled heap. Michael's arm scraped over the asphalt and he gritted his teeth in pain.

"What the heck?" Chris asked. "You trying to kill me?"

"I saw something." Michael crawled up and limped back. Two fifteen-foot skid marks etched the road. He kneeled down and studied them. The pavement burned his knees. "Same tires as the green van. These marks weren't here yesterday." He stood up and followed them to the roadside. Something in the ditch flashed against the sun.

"What?"

Chris appeared beside him and they plodded towards the object. It looked like Katherine's bike.

No. It can't be. Please.

Chris stared, unblinking. His chin quivered.

Michael's heart pounded. He approached the bike. The handlebars were bent and the frame scarred. "Oh my."

Michael spotted Katherine's Saint Christopher necklace lying on the road. He grabbed it and sat beside the bike.

"Makin' this Boy Go Crazy," blared from Chris's phone.

Chris's eyes bugged. He jammed his shaking hand into his pocket and pulled out the phone. He plopped down beside Michael. "It's Katherine," he said. He placed the phone to his ear. "Katherine? Where are you?"

Chris's cheeks flushed. His eyes widened.

"Turn on the speaker," Michael whispered.

Chris selected the speaker. "Who are you?" he asked.

"Not your concern. We've got her, Chris." The voice was deep and gravelly with a thick Scottish accent.

"What? Where? Who are you?"

"You've got one week to put that money back, or she's dead. You call the cops, she's dead. You involve your parents, she's dead. The money, Chris. One week. And no satellite in the world will track her phone, so don't even bother."

The man hung up. Chris dropped the phone.

Michael's intestines slumped like stewed tomatoes.

"What should we do?" Chris asked.
"I...I don't know. Let's go back to our headquarters."

CHAPTER 11

Katherine opened her eyes to black. She could feel her heart pump in her fingertips, her feet, and her scalp.

Her forearm burned. She brushed her hand over it and it felt like warm hamburger rolled in gravel. She clenched her teeth, squeezed a piece of gravel, and popped it out with a burst of sticky blood. She wiped the tears from her eyes and drove her fingers into another one. She pulled the little rocks from her flesh, counting each one. "Thirty," she whispered while pulling the last one out. She laid her head back and panted.

Her cheek throbbed. She poked it and saw a flash of light against the back of her eyelids. Her eyebrow was swollen and her face covered in dry blood. Not broken, she thought.

She lifted her hand and hit a flat surface. "Weird." She drew her fingers over it. *Wood?*

A splinter drove into her skin. "Ouch!" She popped her index finger into her mouth and tasted blood. She grabbed the splinter with her teeth and pulled it out.

She checked her watch, 2:30 PM. Where was Thomas? She had to warn Mom. What if they went after Thomas?

She lifted her knees and they stopped short.

"Huh?"

She pushed her toes forward and scraped them over a rectangular piece of wood.

Was she encased in a box?

Yes.

Had they buried her? Was she in a graveyard?

A roar, a vibration seized the box. It jostled, and shook. Her head rose. Her stomach sank.

What are the noises? A life support system? Are they throwing me under the ground?

She envisioned six feet of earth above her.

Water seeped down and pushed through the cracks in her coffin. It soaked into her jeans. It was freezing. Bugs fought through the loose soil, ate through the wood, and dropped on her legs. They buried into her skin and lay their eggs.

She screamed a piercing, guttural scream of mourning, terror, and hopelessness, as though a giant, flesh-eating bug was dragging her to its lair, the last semblance of daylight fading as its trap door closed on her clawing fingers. She pounded and kicked at her coffin with ear shattering booms.

She was going to die.

"Let me out of here! Please, oh please! Let me out of here!"

She kicked her feet and banged her knees. She panted. Her air supply dwindled. Carbon monoxide seeped into her brain. "No, no, no." She started to sob.

A green fluorescent glow flooded the coffin. "Huh?" She glanced down. A marble of light hovered at her feet.

Her breathing slowed. *Am I in heaven?*

She sighed. The light penetrated her skin, spreading through her legs, into her abdomen, and up through her chest. Her heart rate slowed. Her eyelids drooped. An angel lay down beside her.

"So beautiful."

She sighed in the warmth and drifted off.

CHAPTER 12

Michael was sitting at the table in their headquarters with his head in his arms. He and Chris had been talking for the past two hours, trying to come up with a rescue plan, to no avail. Michael had checked her phone and just like the man said, he couldn't track it.

He heard footsteps outside the door and grimaced.

Thomas burst through the door. "Hey, guys, what's the matter? You look like you've seen a ghost."

A school of piranhas flooded Michael's stomach, flopping, fighting, slicing and dicing. He folded at his waist and rubbed his eyes. They stung.

Thomas stopped. "What?"

Michael lifted his head and stared into Thomas's eyes. They shone back at him. Michael's legs went numb and his heart hurt like it was swollen. His chin started to wobble and he bit into his lip.

"What is it?" Thomas yelled.

Michael heaved. "I'm sorry, Thomas."

"Sorry? About what?"

"Robert Cain. He figured out who took his money."

"What happened?" Thomas said. His eyes darted from Michael to Chris.

"I...I," Michael said.

"What the? Tell me!"

"They've got Katherine."

"Whad'ya mean? Who's got Katherine? I said goodbye to her this morning. She left on her bike." Thomas's face turned crimson.

"Robert Cain."

Thomas stared. "Huh?"

"He's kidnapped her."

Thomas backed into the wall. "How? How did they? How do we get her back?"

"I don't know."

Thomas flopped onto a chair. His chin trembled. "Wha...what...what are they gonna do with her?"

Michael straightened up. "They've given us a week to give the money back."

Thomas lurched forward. "Then give it back!"

Michael glanced at Chris.

"Not until the last day," Michael said.

"No!" Thomas yelped. "Now! Give it back now!"

Michael sighed. "We can't trust them, Thomas. Our best option is to find her."

"Can't trust them to what?"

Chris stood up and sighed. He paced around the room. "We can't trust them to return her."

"No! They have to!"

"We're going to find her," Chris said.

"How? We're just a bunch of kids! We don't know where she is. We don't know where Robert is."

"She's gotta be close. We'll find her," Michael said.

Chris stopped and sat down. "No, I think they're taking her to Robert."

"Huh?"

"I don't know why. I just think they are."

"We have to be sure about these things, Chris," Michael snapped. "We can't go on a hunch. How do you know?"

"I don't. It's just a hunch, a big one."

"Fine then," Thomas said. "Let's go with that. What now?"

"What about her text?" Chris asked.

Thomas jumped from his chair. "She sent a text?"

"Yeah."

"What did it say?"

"Credit card. Help me."

"That makes no sense," Thomas said. "She doesn't have a credit card."

"Who has a credit card then?" Michael said.

"Our parents do."

"Whose parents don't?"

Michael rose from his chair and paced. "Who has a credit card? Who has a credit card?"

"Robert does."

"What was that, Thomas?" Chris asked.

"Robert does. He has a credit card."

"Of course he does. Under Joe Vinte. I tried to pay his account, remember?" Michael said.

"What bills did you pay?" Chris's voice squeaked.

"I don't know," Michael snapped. "Why would I even look?"

Michael saw the glitter in Chris's eyes. He felt his face flush. "I'm an idiot. Hotel bills, of course."

Michael dashed to the computer. Chris and Thomas's chairs crashed onto the floor as they jumped up and followed him.

"I downloaded Robert's statement to my computer." Michael opened up the document and scanned through it. "Let's see."

"Ah-hah! Here it is. Mexico! He's in Mexico guys. Iberostill Hotel. How could I miss that?"

"Great," Chris said, "let's get moving then."

"How do we get to Mexico?" Thomas asked.

"Not sure," Michael said. "But we better leave tomorrow. I'll make reservations at the... "

"Okay guys, slow down. We've been here before," Chris said.

"What?" Michael asked.

"Our parents, we have to tell them."

Thomas stomped his foot. "But they said they'd kill her if we did!"

"They'll do nothing till they get the money. Your mom has to know," Chris said.

Thomas rubbed his eyes. "Yeah, you're right."

Michael stood. "What about the money? Do we tell them?"

Chris stood and walked to the door. "Hmmm...no. Let's just say they're holding her for ransom. The cops find out about the money and they'll take it, and it may come in handy. We'll hire mercenaries if we have to. Come on. Let's go."

They crept down the ladder and shuffled through the barn, shoulders slumped and heads hung like they were condemned.

"I'll tell 'em," Michael said.

"No, Michael, I'm the oldest. I should have known better. I'll tell them."

"Mom's gonna die," Thomas whispered.

CHAPTER 13

Robert Cain took a sip from his martini and placed the phone to his ear. "Pete?"

"Hello? Robert, ah, Geoff."

"Hi, Pete. You got her?"

"Yep. Nailed up in a crate."

"Oh. How's the flight?"

"Going well."

"Is she all right?"

"Been pretty quiet actually. She really freaked out just after we took off."

"Does she have an air supply?"

"Uh, I think the cracks in the wood should do."

"Geez, Pete, I hope you didn't kill her already. Pop the lid off that thing and check her out."

"Uh. Yeah, sure. Are you set?"

"The guest house is ready. Did you tell the kids?"

"Yep. Talked to Chris. Just like you said. Scared the crap out of him."

"Great. We'll get the money then."

"Then what? Do we fly her back?"

"Forget it. Too risky. After we get the cash, do what you want with her. Just make sure she doesn't live through it, okay?"

"Awesome! Right on then. And our flight path? No problems?"

"Friends in high places, Pete. Your flight doesn't exist."

"Okay. Uh, hold on Geoff, something's wrong."

"What?"
"Doh! No."
"What's going on, Pete?"
"Going down! We're going down! Ugh. I can't get them started!"
"Pete! Where are you? Get what started?"
"Shsshhi, mugghh, mountains, trrrrees, nnnnooooo, aaggghhhhhhh!"
"Pete!"

CHAPTER 14

A huge bang snapped Katherine from sleep. She felt like she was on a bobsled hurling through a pitch black tunnel.
Water-slide?

She slammed into the lid and stuck to it. Her stomach plummeted.

"Oh God, they've thrown me off a bridge."

Every conversation, emotion, action, dream, fear, laugh, and tear, from her first memory in life to riding her bike to Chris's house, flashed by in a millisecond, with emotions so powerful that she gasped. She burst into tears. Her mom, Thomas, Chris; she would never see them again. She'd had no chance to say goodbye.

"Thomas! Mom! I'm okay. Please don't worry. I'll miss you.

"Why me? What did I do? God, whatever I've done, I'm so sorry."

The coffin shot forward. She was fired back and her head cracked into the box. "Aggghhh!"

A noise like a tree shredder slammed through the box. She clapped her hands over her ears. Her tendons strummed like guitar strings.

"A tornado?" she wondered.

She crashed to the bottom of the coffin. It accelerated, spun, and flipped end-over-end. The wood ground her flesh like a cheese grater. She screamed and jammed her arms and knees against the box. Her feet hit the end and her ankles cracked. She bit her lip, trying not to pass out.

"Ahhhggggg!"

The box slammed into the ground and shattered into a cloud of splinters. She vaulted towards a fir tree and threw up her arms to protect her head.

Around her, a green bubble formed, as though created from the air she breathed. She slowed, lurched to a stop, floated like a feather, and spun around. She lay on a forest floor. The moss felt cool against her back.

A bright light flooded the sky. She rose to it. It was warm and comforting, like her mother's hug. She flipped over and looked down at herself.

"No!"

Dirt and branches were piled around her body. A mangled and bleeding corpse, she lay on her back while her eyes stared back at her. They were lifeless.

CHAPTER 15

Thomas was crying. Chris sat stone-faced, staring into the wall. They were in the library. Their parents had left for the airport. The police were in the house, talking in the living room. Michael, Chris, and Thomas were told to stay put until their aunt arrived. Michael had never felt more useless in his life. He stood up. "Come on guys, let's get out of here."

"Where?" Thomas asked.

"Headquarters," Michael said. He walked to the library door, opened it, and turned to Thomas and Chris, who were standing behind him, and motioned for them to follow him.

"What about the cops?" Chris whispered.

"Eventually they'll figure out no one's here," Michael said. He stepped out of the library and tiptoed down the hallway to the front door. He opened it, stepped outside and waited for Thomas and Chris. They lumbered down the stairs and onto the driveway. The sun was low in the sky and the trees cast shadows over the yard.

Michael kicked a rock. It skittered over the pavement and banged into one of the four police cruisers parked outside their house. He winced.

"Michael!" Chris said.

Michael kicked another rock. "That didn't go well."

"What did you expect?" Chris asked.

"Yeah, I guess I knew they'd be really mad."

"I can't believe the police won't help us," Thomas said.

"He's got to them," Michael said.

Chris stopped and looked at Michael, tilting his head to the side. "Really, Michael? You think Robert Cain controls the police?"

"I think he controls a lot of things."

"Like what?" Thomas asked.

"Everything governments control, which is everything. The fact is, we can't trust anyone."

Chris shook his head and started walking. "I think you're nuts, Michael."

Their dad, Jane, Greg, and Tracy were on a flight to Mexico. Michael and Chris wanted to go too. They had argued with their dad until he turned red and yelled at them. Thomas didn't have a passport anyway. Michael didn't want to leave him alone.

Thomas crept up the ladder. Michael waved Chris on and then followed him. They plodded to the table and sat down.

Thomas rocked like a patient in an insane asylum.

"Thomas, are you all right?" Chris asked.

"She's my sister," he whispered. He closed his eyes. His chin shook. "She would hide me under the stairs, in the cellar, before the beatings started. I don't know how she knew."

"What?" Chris whispered.

"She took them for me. I didn't even try to help her. She didn't cry or nuthin'."

Chris reached over and placed his hand on Thomas's arm. "Thomas, I...what are you saying?"

Thomas stared at the wall and sang. "This little light of mine, I'm gonna let it shine. This little light of mine, I'm gonna let it shine.

"She'd sing to me after. We'd fall asleep in our cubbyhole. I'd watch the bruises grow on her arms.

"I didn't even try to help her. God, why didn't I help her? I'm such a coward."

"Thomas?" Chris asked. "Are you okay?"

"Fine," Thomas said.

Michael swallowed a lump in his throat. What was Thomas on about? Who else had hurt him, and Katherine? He wanted to walk over and hug Thomas, but he was afraid Thomas would lash out. He glanced at Chris. Chris shrugged his shoulders.

"They were lucky to get a flight," Michael said. He needed to change the subject.

"Someone must have cancelled," Chris said. "How long does it take to fly to Mexico anyway?"

"Seven hours," Thomas said.

Michael and Chris looked over at him. His eyes were red.

"We'll get her back," Michael said.

Thomas jumped up. "What if we don't?" He yelled. "What if they kill her? She's all I've got. And it's your fault, Michael. You shouldn't have taken that money!"

He swung at Michael's head and missed. "It's your fault. I wish I'd never met you and your stupid uncle. I wish you were dead!"

Michael needed to puke. He glanced at the kitchen sink.

Chris walked over and put his arm around Thomas's shoulders. "We'll find her. Don't be mad at Michael. We have to work together."

Thomas pushed Chris away. "How? We're stuck in this stupid hole waiting for my mom and your parents to rescue her. What can we do but wait for her to die?"

"He's right, Chris. We're not doing anything here."

"Well, we're sure not flying to Mexico," Chris said.

Michael jumped up. "Let's track down Robert then, before they land."

Thomas unclenched his fists. "How 'bout I phone the hotel? I'll ask for Robert Cain."

Michael walked to his computer. "Sounds like a good start. Don't ask for Robert though, ask for Joe Vinte. Remember?"

"Right, let me at it then."

"I'll check out Robert's credit card account," Michael said. He sat down at his computer.

Chris turned on Thomas's computer. "Do you want me to talk?"

Thomas sat down in the chair. "No, I will." He wiped his eyes with his sleeve.

"Turn on the synthesizer," Michael said. "Oh, and record it."

Chris grabbed the headset. "Here, Thomas, put these on. I'll dial them up for you." Chris set 'adult male' into the synthesizer and passed the headset to Thomas. Chris used Google to find the number and call it.

A young lady's voice crackled through the speaker. "Iberostill Hotel. How may I direct your call?"

"Front desk, please," Thomas said.

Thomas's chin shook. He was going to cry and blow everything.

His synthesized voice was deep, but it didn't cover the emotion.

"Front Desk. John here. How may I help you?"

"Hello, John. My name is Thomas. I'm calling for Joe Vinte." Thomas bit down on his lip and dropped his head. He sobbed.

"Come on, Thomas," Michael whispered, "concentrate."

"Are you okay, sir?"

"Ye...yes. I have a message for Joe. He gave me his number, but it doesn't work."

"Yes, sir. Joe checked out this morning. He didn't comment on his whereabouts, but he checks in for messages. Do you want to leave one?"

"Uh, no. He'll get back to me. It's, it's important. Are you sure you don't know where he went?"

"Well, between us, I heard from a real estate friend of mine that he purchased a huge ranch in Sonora. I think that's where he went today."

"Do you know where the ranch is?"

"Can't say. Should be easy to find though. Ranches of that extravagance don't sell without a ripple."

"Thanks. You've been a great help. Oh, ah, don't tell him I called, okay? If he finds out I wrote down the number wrong he'll kill me."

"Heh. Not literally, I hope. No problem. I won't tell him."

"Thanks. Bye." Thomas tore off the headset. "Michael?"

"Just a sec." Michael pounded on the keys, zeroing in on luxury ranches recently sold. "Got it. Outside of Huachinera, in the Sierra Madre Mountains. Holy, 21,000 acres. Three houses, one that's six thousand square feet. Eight bathrooms, a gym, putting green, horses, and a landing strip. Couple of swimming pools too."

"Nice of him to invest our inheritance," Chris quipped.

"Yes!" Thomas yelled. "We've got him. Call your dad."

"Can't," Michael said. "Not until they land. Find directions for this place. I'll see if I can hack the estate computers."

CHAPTER 16

The smell, it crawled down Katherine's nose, pushed into her brain, and pricked her senses -- rotting leaves, wet dirt, jet fuel, and smoke.

The wind howled like an old woman in mourning. Water gurgled in the distance, to her right. Birds fluttered and chirped, seemingly concerned with the onslaught of wind.

She hurt -- her eyeballs, her head, her feet, her neck, her arms, her shoulders, her bones, her skin, and where there should have been skin.

Something was sitting on her chest. It tickled her nose and poked her cheeks.

The jet fuel smelled horrible. She curled her lips and gagged. She needed to throw up, but her stomach was empty.

She reviewed the last few seconds before she'd blacked out. They didn't make sense. The green angel and the bubble?

She opened her eyes to a pair of yellow teeth and shivering whiskers. A squirrel; it jumped up, dropped its head, and sniffed her nose.

She wiggled her toes and gasped in pain. They were stiff. She raised her knees. Her calf muscles curled into balls. She screamed and pushed her heels out.

The squirrel ducked and chirped. She raised her right arm and pushed it off.

It scolded her like a misfiring engine and darted away.

"So far, so good," she whispered. She raised her left arm. "Nothing's broken."

She pushed her elbows into the ground and pulled into a sitting position. Her stomach muscles cramped. Black spots swirled through her head and she swooned.

"Oh." She gasped at the pain shooting down her neck and shoulders.

She lay back down.

The forest sounds were beautiful and scary. She listened for a moment then sat up and scanned the terrain. Smoke blanketed the ground like fog in a graveyard.

She was surrounded by fir trees, perhaps one hundred and fifty feet tall, with trunks up to five feet wide. The forest floor was littered with decaying logs and boulders and carpeted in a thick layer of lime-green moss. It was beautiful.

Mountains, perhaps two-thousand feet high and capped with snow covered peaks enclosed her in a valley.

She shivered. Her T-shirt would not keep her warm up here.

She looked behind her. The trees still standing were scarred, their bark torn away like scabs, revealing pinkish wood underneath. Between them was a path of devastation leading back farther than she could see. Smaller trees were broken, scattered, or piled like beaver dams. A dozen little fires billowed yellow smoke.

A flash of white caught her eye. There was something manmade behind a pile of trees about forty feet back. Curious, she rolled over and pushed onto all fours. She leaned onto a rotting log, stood up, and peered at the object. It was too obscured to see.

She stepped forward and grimaced. Her legs were on fire. She looked down to her blood stained jeans, undid them, and tried to pull them down. They stuck to her flesh, and peeled away scabs as she lowered them. Her skin erupted into bubbles of blood. She held her breath and yanked them down past her knees, and fell to the ground screaming. She panted, and cussed her skinny jeans. When the pain wouldn't subside she sat up and checked her legs. Nothing was broken but her skin looked like she'd taken a cheese grater to it. She stood up and ran her hands through her jeans. They were shredded but better than nothing. She prayed, grabbed onto them, pulled them up fast, and blacked out.

Katherine didn't know how long she was out, but it was still daylight. She stood up and fastened her jeans. Her legs were numb. Perhaps she had grown used to the pain. She stepped over a fallen tree and walked to a Nike running shoe.

"Who's?"

She tossed it aside and pressed on.

She stopped. Did she hear a voice? Did someone whisper? Or was it the wind?

She waited and listened. The trees groaned under the onslaught of wind.

She scrambled over a pile of trees and looked under a fallen log at the white object. It was an airplane cockpit. It had snapped from the fuselage and, by the looks of it, rolled down the valley like a soccer ball. She ducked under the log and scrambled to the side of the fuselage. It was buried into the dirt, so she doubled around the back of it and to the other side.

"Gah!" A body hung through the window. A ring of jagged glass cut into his torso. His head was twisted around, his grey eyes wide open, and they stared right at her. She gagged.

She continued, ducking under and climbing over fallen trees. There was another body ahead of her, lying on a bed of moss and twisted and bloody, as though whipped by a blender. She walked up to him and was shocked to see only a stub where his head should have been.

"Oh no." She stared at the stub of flesh. *Where is it?* She jumped and glanced around. "Where?"

She stepped around him, tripped over a stump and fell into a pile of branches. They grazed her skin, scraping away scabs. Pain screamed through her body and bright dots of light circled her head. She bit her lip, fighting to stay conscious.

"Move, Katherine!" She said. "You'll die here." She pushed onto her feet, turned, and stared at the corpse.

"Thank God. Still there," she whispered.

She trudged around a pile of trees. A black object caught her eye and she dashed to it. "A gun."

She picked it up. A holster lay a few feet away. She grabbed it and slung it over her shoulder and strapped it around her waist. She pointed the gun at a tree, turned her head and pulled the trigger, nothing.

She looked for a safety but couldn't find one. It looked like a toy gun Thomas used to play with and on a hunch she placed her hand over the top of the gun at the handle and pulled. It slid back and stopped. She held the gun with two hands, aimed it at a tree with her elbows locked, and squeezed the trigger. The trigger seemed to go back too far. Turning her head away she pulled more. The gun jumped and pushed her wrists back as it fired. The bang echoed down the canyon. She smiled. "Cool." Trembling, she turned and walked up the hill.

Another white object appeared fifty feet ahead of her, the fuselage. She trudged up to it. It lay perpendicular to the path of destruction. It was scratched and scarred and the wings and stabilizers were missing, but the windows weren't broken. She walked to the open hole, where it split from the cockpit and peered inside. There were no seats.

Removed for my coffin.

She giggled at the irony.

The shadows were growing. She shivered and grabbed her arms. "Ouch!"

She looked west. The sun rested on a pointy mountain peak, looking as though it would pop and flood the valley with its insides. Katherine imagined brilliant yellow lava pouring down the mountains. She closed her eyes and smiled.

She peeked at her watch. It was 6:40PM. She had to find a safe place to sleep before dark.

She took a deep breath, turned towards the cockpit, and thought for a moment. She stepped towards it and stopped. It was the last place she wanted to go, but she needed tools.

"Go, Katherine." She climbed over a tree and started towards the cockpit.

She approached from the left, away from the corpse, and scanned the ground as she walked, looking for his head. She really didn't want to find it. The back of the cockpit was torn open like a soup can but covered in broken trees. She grabbed a trunk, just wider than her hands, grunted, and dragged it aside. A hole appeared. She flopped onto her knees and pushed inside, avoiding the jagged edges.

A metal box was attached to the floor behind the copilot's seat. She popped open a latch and looked inside. A hatchet was secured to the bottom, along with a first aid kit, a blanket, a knife, a rope, and some flares.

She swallowed.

Breathing through her mouth, she grabbed the pilot's belt and pulled. Shards of glass dug into his waist, snapping off as she dragged him. She fell to her knees and wretched.

"I so wish I had food in there to puke up."

She grabbed his belt, placed her foot on the instrument panel, and pulled.

"Uh..."

He popped through and fell into his chair. His head remained twisted, and faced the headrest. "God bless your soul."

She held her breath and pushed her hand into his pocket. He was cold. She grabbed his wallet, opened it, and checked his driver's license. "Pete." She tossed it aside. She dug further, felt a piece of plastic and pulled it out, her cell phone.

"Thank goodness," she whispered. "I hope I get reception."

A ball of fur flew through the window into the pilot's lap, and she jumped and screamed. It chittered and chattered at her, and twitched its tail.

"Stupid squirrel! Scared the heck outta me. Jeez. So, you wanna build a shelter?"

She pushed her phone into her pocket, gathered the items from the metal box, wrapped them in the blanket, and carried them back to the fuselage.

She needed tree trunks about two inches in diameter and the plane had chopped up a whole collection of them. She found one a few steps from the fuselage, about six feet long.

"Perfect."

She dragged it to the fuselage, measured it against the opening, and chopped off one end with the hatchet, making it an inch longer than needed. She forced it vertically into the fuselage hole. She ran into the forest, found another, chopped it to size, and jammed it horizontally into the fuselage, making a cross.

She dragged two more trees over, cut them to size, and pushed them into the hole diagonally, forming a frame that looked like a pie cut into eight pieces. She hacked six- foot pieces of rope and lashed the trees together. She stood back and smiled. With the hole plugged she had all the protection she'd need.

Scampering around, she gathered evergreen branches from the forest floor. She weaved them through the frame, plugging the spaces and creating a solid wall, except for a hole at the bottom to crawl through. She covered the wall with the blanket, pushing the edges in to secure it.

"There," she said to the squirrel. "Whad'ya think? I think I'll do just fine in there."

Starlight cast a faint glow through the forest, turning the trees into black monoliths. It was dead quiet, like the cornfields at her grandparents' farm.

She dropped to her knees and felt over the ground, finding the axe, first aid kit, flares and the gun. She placed them into the fuselage and crawled in, working her way to the cargo net at the back. She ran her hands around it, pulling it off the hooks. Two suitcases lay on the floor behind it. She could reach through and grabbed one.

She sat down, unzipped it and felt around inside. "Yes!" She grabbed the flashlight and switched it on. The suitcase was filled with shorts and T-shirts. They must have been taking her to a warm climate. "I need something warmer than that."

She tossed the suitcase back behind the net and pulled out a second one. She unzipped it and found some shorts and two white dress shirts. A bottle of Naya Springs water lay under the shirts, like a brick of gold. She grabbed it, whipped off the top, and pressed it to her lips, sucking the water so hard the bottle popped. Her throat was sore and the water felt like fire against it.

She set the bottle aside, turned to the suitcase, and pulled out a broken cardboard box. "Fifty rounds," she read. She grabbed a handful of bullets from the bottom of the suitcase. They were heavy and cold.

She found a toiletry bag and unzipped it. Inside was a bar of soap, a tube of toothpaste, a shaver, and two granola bars. She grabbed one of the bars, tore off the wrapper, and broke off a small piece and tossed it to the squirrel. She bit into the bar and her stomach growled.

"Go home, buddy or I'll make fur gloves out of you," she said as she shooed the squirrel out the door.

She covered the entrance with a suitcase and pulled a candle and matches from the first aid kit. She struck a match against the floor and placed it against the wick of the candle, which hissed and spit like a cat. Light flickered through the fuselage, casting ghostly shadows. She giggled. She should be a ghost right now.

She flicked on the flashlight and popped open her cell phone.

Two bars remained on the battery display.

A faint noise outside caused the hair on her arms to spring up. She placed the phone down, crawled to the door and poked her head out. Wolves yipped in the distance. She trembled. The excitement in their yips and howls reminded her of a pack of hyenas she'd seen on TV that had chased down a zebra and torn it to pieces.

The valley fell quiet and she could hear only the wind again.

A cold breeze blew through the cracks in her door and she shivered. The candle flickered.

A wolf howled. It was a long and lonely sound and made Katherine feel even more despondent. She was a protector and needed someone to protect right now. She'd never forgive Michael for taking that away from her. How many years had Thomas endured Michael, and she hadn't been there for him? He got to Thomas without going through her first. She clenched her fists.

She was struck with an idea.

She grabbed the flashlight and crawled through the door. Pointing the flashlight at her feet, she picked her way through the forest until she reached the cockpit, and crawled into it.

"Gah." The body smelled putrid. She plugged her nose and squeezed by the pilot. She directed the flashlight at the console, studying each dial and gauge.

The wolves were barking. Funny, she didn't know wolves barked, and it sounded like they were twenty feet away.

"Come on, Katherine. Find it! she yelled.

"There!"

Her flashlight lit up a set of numbers inside a dial, like a car speedometer. Below them was the word 'Elevation'. She whispered the numbers to herself, cementing them into memory.

"2100."

The light flashed against a gold band on the pilot's wrist.

"A watch?"

The crystal was shattered. The arms were still.

"3:10PM," she whispered.

She backed out and hopped to the ground. She could hear the wolves pant, and their footsteps on the moss. They were running. She started to hyperventilate. She dashed towards the fuselage, leaping over and under trees, ignoring the pain they inflicted. She imagined wolf teeth tearing into her flesh and she started to sob.

The fuselage was just beyond the flashlight beam. She jumped over a fallen tree and sprinted. She fell.

The footsteps had stopped. She crouched and listened to the wind. A throaty growl drifted from the trees and she shuddered. She pointed the flashlight towards the growl and a pair of lights shone back at her. They moved down and up, and drifted towards her. A wolf crept into view, twelve feet to her right. It dropped its nose to the ground and sniffed. It was the color of cream. Its feet were as large as baseball gloves. It was six feet long.

"Huge," she whispered.

The wolf bared its teeth and growled.

She jumped up and ran, screaming. She dove into the fuselage, pulled in her feet, and threw the suitcase at the hole. She pointed the flashlight out the window at her right. Three wolves paced along the fuselage. She could hear sniffing at the door, and she whimpered and shimmied to the back of the plane. The suitcase fell over and a massive, black head sprung through her wall. It snapped and growled and bared its teeth. The wall screeched over the metal fuselage as the wolf pushed against it.

Katherine screamed.

The gun? Where's the gun? She threw herself down and felt along the floor. The wolf was four feet from her head. The wall buckled and snapped. She knocked the water bottle over and it glugged onto the floor.

"I found it, you son of a bitch!" She swung the nozzle at the wolf and armed it. "Go away!"

It lunged.

She closed her eyes and squeezed the trigger.

She had heard a twenty-one-gun salute before. It was the loudest noise she'd ever heard and her ears had hurt all day, but it was nothing compared to this. Her eardrums screamed like they had burst. The smell of gunpowder stung her nose. The gun recoiled and cracked into her forehead. She saw stars. She opened her eyes to black. She swept her hands over the floor and brushed the flashlight. She tried to pick it up, but her hands were shaking and she couldn't close her fingers around it.

"Come on, Katherine!"

She squeezed the flashlight and turned it on. The wolf was gone. Did she hit it?

Feet scattered outside. The wolves growled, nipped, and whined. Something tore and cracked. She listened to them for ten minutes.

The forest grew silent. She crawled to the wall, put her feet against it, and pushed it back into place.

She picked up her phone, punched out a text message, and sent it to Chris. Michael had purchased them satellite phones, another brilliant idea. She had full reception.

"I hope he gets this," she whispered. She missed him.

She armed the gun, put her finger through the trigger, and pointed it at the door, resting her arms on her knees.

She heard a loud yawn, a crack, and a crescendo of snapping branches. She threw her hands over her head.

Ku-whump!

The fuselage leapt off the ground. She screamed.

"Missed," she whispered.

She listened to her watch tick and stared at the door. She thought back to Chris's face when she yelled at him. He looked so hurt. How could she have been so mean? Seconds turned to hours. Her eyelids grew heavy. The gun fell to the floor and hit the rug with a thump. The candle sputtered.

CHAPTER 17

Tracy sat at a table so tiny her knees were wedged underneath it. She was locked in a room not much bigger than the table. The walls, ceiling, table, chair, and floor were white, and only a mirrored window no bigger than a sheet of writing paper broke the visual monotony. She stared into the tabletop, uncomfortable that someone may be looking into her eyes without her permission. Frustration raced through her nervous system and accumulated in her feet. She tapped the cheap, tiled floor with an un-patterned beat.

She was exasperated with the wait, of containing her emotions, of pretending to be calm and unconcerned.

She jumped up. Her chair struck the wall. Her legs drove into the underside of the desk. "Let me out of here!"

She sat down and placed her head in her hands.

Her children were her pride and joy. She'd worked tirelessly to give them all she could afford -- a home, an education, a Christmas present every year. She was driven to make up for the abuse they'd suffered as children, to overcome the guilt that haunted her. Why hadn't she seen the monster before they were married? She recollected that cold February night. "Where are we going?" Katherine and Thomas had asked with tiny voices. "Ssshh, we'll be fine," she'd said. She'd bundled them up in what little clothes their father had allowed them, and crept out of the house before he'd gotten back from the bar.

They'd hopped a Greyhound to Silvertip. Her children had slept. They'd looked so fragile under the moonlight. She'd sat upright, biting her fingernails and watching them.

It has to be better, she had thought.

They'd walked from the bus stop to a woman's shelter -- a small and disheveled home, buried within rows of old houses, many splashed with graffiti. They'd shuffled up a brick sidewalk and Tracy had knocked on a purple door. The door had cracked open. They'd been greeted by a pair of dancing, blue eyes; an old woman with a crinkled face and white hair. She'd buried her eyes in a smile and had looked at Tracy as though expecting her. "Hello, my name is Stella," she'd said. She'd given Tracy a long hug. She'd crouched to the floor, her bones audibly creaking, and swayed. Tracy had lowered her hands in preparation to catch her. Stella had hugged Thomas, and then Katherine, and had said in a hushed voice, "You'll be fine here."

Tracy had cried.

Stella had found a school for Katherine and had looked after Thomas while Tracy found a job. She'd cooked breakfast and supper, and fresh chocolate chip cookies every Friday evening.

A lump welled in Tracy's throat as she recalled the day they had left.

Stella had passed away soon after, God bless her soul.

"Why won't you let me go? What do you want?" Tracy whispered.

Border authorities had pulled her, Jane, Greg, and Geoff aside as they had left the plane. Had someone bribed them?

It was ten in the morning. They had interrogated her for three of the past four hours. She had asked for water and to go to the bathroom. They permitted her neither.

Katherine was held by captors, doing God knows what to her. Thomas was at home, wallowing in fear and hopelessness beyond that ever felt by most twelve year old children. She was stuck here, useless.

The door opened with a sickening squeak. Tracy jumped. A uniformed officer snapped into the room and glanced at her with a polished sneer. "Come with me."

Tracy crawled over the desk. The officer grabbed her arm and pushed her down a hallway. Painted yellow, it seemed too cheerful. They came to a door, a yellowed, dirty, and faded door with a worn, brass handle. The officer opened it and shoved Tracy into a room. It smelled like sweat and cigarettes. Geoff, Jane, and Greg were inside with their feet shackled and strapped to chairs. They looked at her with eyes devoid of all emotion but fear. An officer stood behind them with his hands behind his back.

Firing squad? Her heart thumped against her ribcage.

The officer walked Tracy to an empty chair at the end, beside Jane. "Sit."

She sat down. The officer pulled a pair of handcuffs from a leather pouch on his waist and snapped them around her ankles, while the officer from behind pulled a canvas strap around her chest, cinched it up, and tied it around the back of the chair.

The door opened. Robert sauntered in.

"Robert," Greg whispered.

Jane twisted against her restraints. Her chair scraped over the floor. "You jerk!" She shouted. "How could you? Where is she? Where is she! What have you done to her?"

Robert smiled. "That's no way to talk to your brother."

"You're no brother of mine!" Jane yelled.

Robert smirked. "She's safe, for now."

"She has nothing to do with this," Tracy said. "Why?"

"Oh, she has lots to do with it now," Robert said. He walked to Jane and knelt until his face was inches from hers.

"No kids. You knew the rules. I told you."

"You have no right," Jane whispered.

Robert sneered. "Rights are for wimps." He walked away and grabbed a chair, dragged it to Jane, placed it backwards in front of her, and sat down, leaning on the chair back.

"You touch her, I'll hunt you down and kill you," Greg said.

Robert smiled. "Oh, you do that Greg. That would be fun."

He looked at Jane. "You can get Katherine back, Jane. You can get her back to her mommy." Robert glanced at Tracy and smiled, and looked back at Jane. "Chris and Mike, give them to me. I'll give you Katherine. After all, this is your fault. I told you not to have children and you ignored me. Can you live with Katherine on your conscience?"

"You are a jerk," Geoff muttered.

Jane looked to the floor and sobbed.

"Don't," Tracy said. "I would never expect you to do that."

"Oh, aren't you a martyr," Robert said. "It's easy when it's not your life, isn't it?"

"I'd take my life for my daughter's, any day, you jerk. But you wouldn't know love like that, would you?"

Robert stood up and marched to Geoff. His face grew taught. "And I want that machine."

"I can't give it to you," Geoff said. "It's not mine."

"Oh, no worries there Geoff, I'm taking it. Just tell me how."

Geoff looked at Tracy.

She could feel her tears running down her cheeks, and wished she could wipe them off.

"I'll give you the machine, you leave the kids alone," Geoff said.

Robert grabbed the chair, dragged it in front of Geoff, and sat down. "Okay, now you're talking. I'll consider that. How do I get it?"

"How do I get the kids," Geoff asked.

"You're in no position to barter with me!" Robert yelled. "How do I get it?"

Geoff hung his head to the floor. He looked up at Robert. "It's on the top floor of the tallest building in the compound. It weighs four tons, but it's designed to be moved. It's latched to the floor with snap catches. The breakers are in a small room beside it. Throw the breakers. The power cables are quick connects. Just pull them off. It's underneath a skylight designed to fit it. The skylight can be removed with a crane. Now, give Katherine back, and keep our kids out of this."

Robert stood up and walked to the door. "You'll get your passports in one week."

"What?" Geoff said. "We need them. We can't get back without them."

"Next week," Robert said.

"Why?" Jane said.

Robert smiled. "I've got a plane to catch, and kids to hunt." He glanced at the officers. "Release them in ten minutes." He marched to the door.

"We had a deal!" Geoff yelled.

Robert stopped. He turned and looked over all of them. He smiled. "Surely, you know better than that, Geoff. Nothing will stop me. Michael and Chris know why I have Katherine. Only they can save her."

"No!" Tracy yelled.

Robert looked at her. His blue eyes were like cold steel. "Oh yes," he said. He turned and walked out the door.

"The children," Geoff whispered. "We have to call them."

CHAPTER 18

Michael shuffled to the edge of his chair. "Hey guys, look at this."

"What?" Chris asked.

"I hacked into the estate security system, the estate Robert just bought. You should see this place."

Thomas and Chris dashed over to the computer.

Michael switched through the cameras. The swimming pool was kidney shaped, made with green and white tiles, and had a bar on the side. The kitchen stove was massive, with a stainless steel hood and a dozen gas burners. The dining room table, polished leaf with inlaid gold trim, was surrounded by thirty chairs.

"Wow," Chris said.

"The whole place is controlled through a computer," Michael said. "I can lock or unlock any door I want." Michael switched to a camera, revealing a room with a single cot. He panned around it. The walls were concrete and painted white. There was one open window, secured with bars.

"If they put her in there," Michael said, "I could get her out easy."

Chris's phone blared out the Dylan Scott tune.

Michael jumped and swung around. Chris and Thomas stared, open mouthed as the phone vibrated on the table.

"Get it!" Michael yelled.

Chris snatched it up and stared at the display.

"Katherine?" Michael asked.

"Uh, yes." Chris whispered.

Michael vaulted behind Chris's shoulder.

"What does it say?" Thomas squeaked.

"I...I," Chris said.

"Get a hold of yourself, Chris. What does it say?" Michael demanded.

"I need a pad and a pen," Chris whispered.

"Sit down, Chris." Michael pulled back a chair, ran to his computer, and grabbed a pen and pad. He tossed them onto the table. "Write it down."

PlnCrshed PilotsDead LostInVally Runs north to south Shelter No food Sunset8PM FlyTim1/2Hr LoBat Big fir trees. 2100ftelev. Snocap Mntains Citation CJ3 HlpMe. No worries Thomas, I'm fine. Love you.

"What the heck?" Thomas asked.

Michael felt a stab of hope. "The plane crashed," he whispered.

Thomas turned ashen. His eyes danced back and forth between Michael and Chris. His mouth opened and then closed.

"Relax, Thomas," Michael said. "At least she's not with Robert. She's got a better chance of surviving where she is. We have to find out where though. Chris, let her know we got the message."

Michael hopped in front of his computer, started Google Earth, and zoomed onto North America.

"Okay, they left Silvertip and were on their way to Mexico. They flew for half an hour in a CJ3 Citation Jet."

"I'll check the cruising speed," Thomas said. He jumped up and ran to his computer.

Michael knew the answer but he waited.

"Four hundred eighty miles an hour."

"Thanks, Thomas. 'Bout two-hundred and fifty miles then. Possibly less, being it takes a few minutes to get to cruising speed. Let's draw a two-hundred and fifty mile radius around Silvertip."

Michael measured the distance on Google Earth, popped open the drawing tools, and drew a red circle on the map.

"Great," Chris said, "anywhere between Alberta and Washington."

"Hold on, Chris. She gave us one more clue, sunset at eight. Dunno how accurate that is. She's in a valley."

Michael turned on the sunrise utility. A shadow covered the east side of the map.

"Google Earth shows sunrise and sunset. All we have to do is enter in 8PM. Hmmm...it's gonna be tough to pinpoint with the mountain peaks. He adjusted the time to 7:45PM and then to 8:30PM while watching the night time shadow. He frowned.

"Sunset times change about forty minutes over the state of Montana. If she's in a valley, she could be out by fifteen minutes, easy. I think she's in Washington, or maybe Montana, but we need more information. Chris, ask Katherine to get us more. See if she can climb a mountain and find some landmarks. Thomas, take over here. Search all the mountain ranges above and below this circle. Look for ones that run north to south and are at an elevation of twenty-one hundred feet. I'm going to print this area out on the plotter. Circle the valleys you find with a red marker."

Chris jumped up and started for the door. "I'll prepare some backpacks for a hike."

"Good idea, Chris," Michael said. "Complete a shopping list while you're at it. I'll map out driving routes and check for road closures."

"It's ten o'clock guys," Chris said. "Let's work till midnight. We'll need sleep. We're going on a trip tomorrow. Oh, and I better text Dad and let him know what's happened. They'll have to come back."

"We're not going to wait for them are we?" Thomas asked.

"No way. We have to find her quickly. If her cell runs out before we get there we don't have a hope in, uh...well, yah...it'll be harder to find her." Chris turned and dashed out the door.

CHAPTER 19

Rapid-fire chirping burst through the fuselage. Katherine jumped to her feet and slammed her head into the ceiling. "Ow! Stupid squirrel."

"Where am I?" She felt above her head and down along the plastic fuselage walls. Her fingers brushed a window. It felt like a bag of ice. She shivered.

She recalled herself flying towards the tree...and the green bubble. Where did that bubble come from? Her body had been lying on the forest floor and she'd been above, looking at it. How?

She dropped to her knees, and her scabs cracked open.

"Ow-ow-ow!" She clamped her jaw, held her breath, and waited for the pain to subside. It didn't.

She pawed over the prickly rug. Her fingertips hurt like bees were stinging them. She felt the flashlight, picked it up, and turned it on.

The windows glittered against the white light. Curious, she leaned closer. They were smeared in frozen wolf drool and it scattered the light into prisms. She shrunk away and shuddered. Animal food. It was the most helpless feeling in the world. What if they had reached her? She would have been torn to pieces.

She leaned over, rested her head onto her arms and sobbed. She had seen the light. She would never forget it. It was so beautiful, so warm, and filled with love. Had she died for a few seconds? What if she had gone into it? Would she be in this much pain?

The fuselage was small and cold, like a cellar. The aroma of stale potatoes and onions dug itself from a heap of distant memories. She missed her brother so much.

The squirrel popped through the door and scolded her like an alarm clock.

"I'll turn you into wolf food if you don't shut up. Geez, 6:00AM? Could you have woken any earlier, you little brat?

"Oh well, at least you weren't invited to dinner last night."

She closed her eyes and rocked. She imagined a warm beach under a blistering hot sun with the sound of waves crashing into the sand as she drifted in and out of sleep.

Katherine woke. It was pitch black. Her teeth chattered and she shivered. She recalled a school field trip in Grade 3; they'd toured an industrial meat locker. It had been dark and freezing, and she'd been so terrified of being locked into it that she'd clutched her teacher's arm during the whole tour. This was much worse.

She felt around the floor, grabbed her phone, and popped it open. It was 7:30AM. She read Chris's text. "Good, they got it."

She closed the phone and turned on the flashlight. The squirrel was still at the door. "Hey, Snoopy. I have to go on a hike. I wonder if they registered a flight plan? You'd think they'd have to, though I suppose rules don't apply to kidnappers. I bet you only my gang knows I'm here. Man, I sound like a frog. How 'bout we find some water, Snoopy. Yeah, Snoopy. I like that name for you."

She poked her head out the door and gasped. The night sky was like a cloak of blue velvet with the curve of the atmosphere visible, as though she was inside a glass dome. The stars were brilliant and so thick they looked like clouds of diamonds. The snow-capped peaks on the west side of the valley were a brilliant gold, captured in the first rays of the rising sun, but the east side of the valley was black. Light crept through the valley, giving the trees form, black and menacing with arms of jagged branches and ragged clothes of old man's beard. Never before had she felt so at peace while so afraid.

"Thank you, God," she whispered.

A fallen tree lay alongside the fuselage. It was three-feet thick and would have squashed her like a marshmallow.

Her stomach growled.

She popped out and gathered twigs, bark, old man's beard, and branches from the forest floor. She piled the old man's beard and some twigs into a bowl shaped hollow on a flat rock, just down from the fuselage. She struck a match and placed it under the pile, cupped her hands, and gently blew on it. She added more moss and grass to the small flame, nursing it to a foot high. She placed some evergreen branches in and it flared up.

Chris had taught her how to light a fire. Funny, she'd wondered why at the time.

The flames danced like ballerinas, and warmed her face and caressed her hair. The cold crawled from her bones and she smiled.

Warm, she turned from the fire and shuffled back to the fuselage, crawled in, grabbed the water bottle, and strapped on the gun. She checked the fire before heading west towards the river.

The trees were smaller and the ground was covered with bushes that reached up past her head. The river was loud and Katherine guessed it was within one hundred feet. She pushed into the bushes. They clawed at her scars. She stumbled over a rock and fell to her knees, sending lightning bolts of pain through her legs. She squealed and started to cry.

"Come on, Katherine; get it together, what kind of bushes are these?" She looked up and peered around.

"Green alder, oh, and black elderberry."

She wiped the tears off her cheeks, stood up, and pressed on.

The sun had worked its way through the entire valley. The stumps and dead trees looked like zombies. Her skin erupted into goose flesh. She pushed the visions away.

"River. Find the river."

She stepped forward, slipped on a rock, hit the ground, and tumbled into a ravine.

"Nooagghh!"

She vanished into a canopy of leaves the size of soccer balls and slid under spiked branches, long and round like giant tarantula legs. Pummeling her feet into the dirt to halt her ascent, she lurched to a stop inches from a dense patch of devil's club.

The branches were twice her height and the wind battered the leaves, pushing the spikes within an inch of her nose.

She swallowed and clenched her fists. The thorns pierced her jeans and rested against her legs. They weren't painful, but they threatened to gore her at her first move.

"Relax, Katherine."

She slowed her breathing and relaxed her hands, arms, and legs. She was hidden from the world, buried under the monster leaves and spiny branches. She couldn't stand or turn over to crawl. She couldn't remember if the thorns were poisonous or not. Either way, if stuck with a thousand needles, she wouldn't do so well.

"Devil's club," she said. "Aptly named."

"Okay, slowly now."

She lifted her stomach, pushed her feet into the ground, and wiggled her shoulders up, like a caterpillar. The spikes clawed across her jeans. She stopped and panted.

She saw a flash of green to her left and twisted her neck to look. A garter snake came into focus. It slithered towards her face and stopped at her nose. She held her breath. Its forked tongue flickered over her cheek. Perhaps sensing she was pinned down, it helped itself to her body, slithering over her neck and under her T-shirt. She gasped and winced. She clenched her fists. It wiggled to her stomach, stopped, and poked her bellybutton with its nose. She stifled a scream. It slid down and popped out from under her T-shirt; its weight leaving her as it dropped to the ground.

She raised her stomach again and pushed her shoulders up another inch. "Again, Katherine."

She inched her way up the ravine until she had a foot of clearance, turned over, and crawled out. She stood up and pushed through the green alders.

"Stupid. Trying to get yourself killed?"

Breaking through the bushes she came to the edge of a river. It was over twenty feet wide and a foot deep. She knelt down, filled the bottle, and added a drop of iodine from the first aid kit.

She plunged back into the underbrush, and pushed on for fifty feet, discovering a patch of black gooseberry bushes. "*Ribes lacustre.*" She grinned. Botany was one of her favorite subjects. Her friends thought plants were boring. She found angiosperms, gymnosperms, bryophytes, and pteridophytes to be fascinating, though she didn't expect her hobby to feed her. She stripped the berries from the bushes and dropped them into her mouth. They were bland and slimy. She gorged until she was full and feeling a little sick.

She picked up a branch that was about five feet long and broke the twigs off it, forming a walking stick.

Snoopy's chatter broke through the forest. He was far away but she could discern the direction. Katherine grinned and pushed ahead.

Katherine walked back into the crash site and to the fuselage. She looked above the trees to the snow capped peaks. Clouds formed, whipped, and vanished into the snow cap, only to materialize again. Though certainly as big as a house, they appeared tiny from the valley.

"I have to get up there, Snoopy. The boys need information."

She crawled into the fuselage, grabbed a long sleeve shirt and spread it out on the floor. She tossed in a ball of dry moss and some sticks, matches, the first aid kit, a pen, a sheet of paper, and the water bottle.

"Something to melt snow in," she whispered as she scanned the inside of her shelter.

"Ah-hah!" She dug her fingernails under a metal ashtray imbedded in the side of the fuselage wall and popped it out.

"Tools of a filthy, disgusting, cancer causing addiction finally put to a good use, Snoopy. Thank goodness no one used it."

She opened a suitcase and rummaged around. "Ah-hah." She pulled on a red T-shirt, a green one, and a long sleeve dress shirt, which hung on her like a potato sack. She wrapped up the shirt of goodies, and tied it to the walking stick.

"Huckleberry Finnette, with a gun."

She grinned and crammed a handful of bullets and the cell phone in her left pants pocket, the pocket knife in her right, and buckled the gun holster across her chest.

It was almost eleven. The sky was bright blue and clear. With a spirited gait, she headed east.

Wet strands of hair stuck to Katherine's face. She swept them away, peered around, and frowned. The ground was hard. The spongy moss had vacated the forest floor, driven away by rocks and hard dirt. It was steep and her feet hurt. She couldn't see into the valley through the trees, but she felt she was over a thousand feet above it.

She had been hiking for two hours. The trees were scraggly, short, and sparse as though giving up the effort required to grow. The early morning sun hadn't reached her yet. The air was cool against her sweaty skin.

A noise broke her thoughts. She turned and listened. *Gurgling?*

She walked to her left, and through a patch of crowberry shrubs. She leapt over a fallen log. A creek, barely three feet in width, cascaded down the mountain side. She plunked down beside it, pulled out her water bottle, and guzzled what was left.

She leaned her stick against a rock, rested on her knees, and dipped the water bottle in. She thought of her mom's company picnic, plunging her hand into the ice chest to pull out an orange pop. She shivered and frowned. Mom must be worried sick, she thought.

The bottle filled, she pulled it out and buffed her frozen fingers over her legs. She reached for the iodine. Something caught her eye. It lay motionless and low to the ground behind a rock on the opposite side of the river. Its coat...*mustard?* It blended into the grass, rocks, and bark. Katherine held her breath and stared. She scanned the outline. A recognizable form broke through. She placed the bottle on the ground, without moving her eyes from the form.

Mountain lion!

Katherine had studied mountain lions at school. They were unpredictable and dangerous. She had guessed, by the odd behavior of the wolves, that it had been a tough winter. This creature, like others in the valley, could be hungry.

She lay still and watched it crawl towards her. It broke the trees, twenty feet away. It could leap that in one bound. It would be on her before she could squeak.

She lowered her right arm, unbuckled the gun holster, and pulled out the gun. She engaged it, pointed it at the mountain lion's chest, and stared along the barrel.

Funny, she thought. She'd considered guns to be tools of death. She realized just how wrong she was. Held between her trembling hands, the gun was life. Her life.

The mountain lion stared, licked its lips, and wiggled its hind quarters ever so slightly.

"Go ahead, Tigger. Make my day."

CHAPTER 20

Michael soared through a forested valley. The life-crushing drop to the ground didn't concern him. His arms were spread like an eagle riding an updraft, searching for a delicious rabbit. He grinned. This is so cool.

He swooped towards a snow-capped mountain. It towered above the ground with strength that warped the fabric of space and time. The mountain grew as he approached. Details became clear; scraggily and wind swept trees at the base; large granite rocks, laid by a disastrous avalanche triggered in a distant past; towering granite cliffs soaring thousands of feet into the air; an emerald lake set under the peak.

Snow rolled off the peak in globs, like ice cream drooling down a cone. It plummeted and crashed into the trees at the base, snapping them like tooth picks.

The mountain was mourning. Strange, Michael thought, how can a mountain mourn? Sure enough, like a child's cry pushes fear into the souls of those around her, the mountain projected despair, as though gripping its last remnants of life.

"Michael, wake up."

"Huh?"

"Wake up, it's eight o'clock."

Michael looked to his left. Chris was standing by his bed, fully dressed in a teal T-shirt and blue jeans. His eyes were ringed with black circles. He looked like hell.

Michael's stomach twisted. He needed to cry and squeezed his eyes tight. It was like the morning after his mother had died. His heart ached with grief, with guilt, for this was entirely his fault. He didn't know what he would do if Katherine were to die. Could he live with himself? Could he look at Thomas again?

No, couldn't.

He sat up and rubbed his eyes. "Eight o'clock? Dad? Did he call?"

"Nope. Don't get it. He should have read my text by now. And he's not answering my calls either."

Michael jumped out of bed and pulled on his jeans and T-shirt. Chris walked across the room to Thomas's sleeping bag, grabbed the end of it, and pulled it across the hardwood floor.

Thomas's head popped out. He rubbed his eyes and yawned. "What's up?"

"Let's go get your sister," Chris said.

Thomas sat up. "You know where she is?"

"Not yet. I hope we'll get a text soon. But we can prepare in the mean time."

"How?"

"Take the horses to Rod's, get supplies."

"What about the three spots I found?" Thomas asked. "Can't we just go to one of them? There's a chance we'll pick the right one."

"I thought of that," Michael said. "But they're a few hours away from each other and we've got lots of computer power here. I'd rather not take the chance."

Thomas frowned and climbed out of his sleeping bag. He was fully dressed.

"Aunt Sylvia's here, by the way," Chris said. "She's making breakfast."

Michael dashed to the door. "Thought I could smell breakfast." He ran down the stairs, two at a time. Chris and Thomas thumped after him. Michael skidded into the kitchen. "Hmmm, bacon and eggs."

Aunt Sylvia was at the stove. Her hair was a faded yellow and her cheeks were sagged and wrinkled, but her blue eyes were still as sharp as glass. She had always been skinny, but today she looked frail.

She turned and smiled with her whole face.

"Hi, Aunt Sylvia," Michael said, trying to sound cheerful. "When did you get in?"

"About one this morning. I'm cooking up a nice breakfast. After we do the dishes, we can kick up some excitement."

She had a cool British accent. Michael loved it.

"It'll be easy finding excitement today," Michael said. He grinned and gave his Aunt a hug.

"Are you taking the horses for a ride today or are you going to disappear into that silly fort?" Aunt Sylvia asked. She passed Chris a plate of bacon and eggs. "Pancakes are on the island."

"Uh, a little bit of both, I think," Chris said. "By the way, have you heard from Dad?"

"Nope. It's strange," Aunt Sylvia said. They told me they'd call as soon as they landed. They were scared you guys would do something stupid."

"Hah!" Chris said, a little too forcefully. Aunt Sylvia turned and stared at him with a raised eyebrow. She passed a plate of bacon and eggs to Michael. He passed it to Thomas and took another.

Michael's stomach rumbled. He hopped up onto the cherry wood bar stool, grabbed a piece of bacon and crunched into it. His taste buds hurt.

Chris grabbed three pancakes, tossed them on his plate, and drenched them in maple syrup. "I'm so hungry I could eat a mountain lion. Thanks, Aunty."

"Easy, Chris," Aunt Sylvia said. "It's not going to be your last meal this week."

"I'm not so sure about that," Michael mumbled.

Michael was chasing egg yolk around his plate with a scrap of toast when Chris's cell phone rang. Chris grabbed the phone from the counter top, ran to the library, and slammed the door.

"Thanks for cutting us out," Michael yelled. *Why do they always call him?*

Michael hopped off his stool. "Come on, Thomas, let's do the dishes."

"I'll wash, you dry," Aunt Sylvia said.

Michael grabbed a coffee cup from the drying rack and pushed his T-towel into it. "Last one, Aunt Sylvia."

For once he was glad his aunt refused to use the dishwasher. It was comforting to dry dishes and talk. He turned the T-towel around until it squeaked. He heard the library door open.

Chris strode in and passed the phone to Aunt Sylvia. He waved Michael and Thomas on and scuttled by them towards the front door. Michael placed the cup on the counter and ran after him.

"What took you so long?" Michael asked. "What did they say?"

Chris pulled open the front door. "Lots." He stepped out. Michael and Thomas ran to either side of him.

"Let me guess," Thomas said. "They want us to wait for them."

"Nope."

Michael hopped in front of Chris and walked backwards. "What then?"

"Dad told us to go get her."

"Really?"

"Yep. They can't get out of Mexico for a week. Authorities took their passports."

Michael tripped and stumbled backwards, and turned to walk beside Chris. "Why?"

"Robert."

Michael stopped. "What?"

"Robert. He's coming after us. Dad wants us and Aunt Sylvia to bug out."

They reached the woodwork shop, and the hot air was filled with the smell of stain and varnish. "You think he'll go after us personally?" Michael asked.

"Doubt it, but if he's mad, who knows what he'll do."

Thomas glanced at Chris. "You think he'll try and kill us himself?"

"Maybe. Let's hope he's no better than his minions."

Michael clamped his teeth and looked into the sky. He felt angry and exhilarated. "So now we get to rescue Katherine...and kill Robert."

"Kill Robert?" Thomas asked.

"Put him in jail, I mean," Michael said.

"Let's not worry about Robert," Chris said. "We have to get Katherine."

"I'm good with that," Thomas said.

Chris unlatched the gate. Eight feet wide, it was made with skinny trees and barbed wire. Michael and Thomas stepped back as he pulled it open. They each grabbed a bridle from a shelter beside the gate and walked into the pasture.

"What about Aunt Sylvia?" Michael asked.

"She needs to vanish," Chris said.

Michael hopped over a gopher hole. "Where?"

"Anywhere, but her home."

"Wow," Thomas said. He had a spring in his gait. "So we just have to wait till we hear from Katherine and go get her. Sounds simple enough."

"Let's go," Chris yelled. He broke into a run.

The pasture was rectangular, about ten acres, and bordered by forest on three sides and the river to the north. The horses stood at the southeast corner in the shade, eating clover. Greg and Jane had built the pasture and had bought the horses soon after Michael and Chris's mom had died.

The green grass reached past Michael's knees and it nipped at his skin as he ran. He imagined orange spiders with shiny black legs leaping from the grass and crawling up his shorts. He squirmed as he ran, relieved that Chris and Thomas were in front as he must have looked foolish. The horses reared back a few steps.

Chris and Thomas slowed to a walk. Michael ran up beside Chris. He made long strides and watched his steps. The last thing he needed was to trip over a gopher hole.

Chris moved to the left towards Gravy and Thomas tiptoed to Biscuit on the right. Michael slipped up to Racer. "Easy, boy." He ran his hand down Racer's mane. Racer was his favorite horse. He was chocolate brown with a golden mane and a white diamond on his forehead, and he seemed to listen when Michael talked. When not on the computer, Michael was in the pasture telling Racer about his ideas for inventions. He slid the bridle on. "Got Racer."

"Got Biscuit," Thomas replied.

"Got Gravy," Chris yelled.

Chris led Gravy to Michael and stepped beside Racer with his hands cupped. Michael placed his foot into Chris's hands and hopped onto Racer's bare back. "Thanks, Chris."

Chris helped Thomas onto Biscuit and then jumped onto Gravy.

Michael nudged Racer with his heels and the horse broke into a gallop. He steered Racer around the gopher patch. "Let's go!"

They thundered over the pasture, through the gate, and turned left down the old logging road towards their neighbor, Rod's place.

Michael placed Aunt Sylvia's suitcase into the trunk of her VW Beetle. "Anything else, Aunt Sylvia?"

"No thanks, Michael. That's it."

Chris opened the driver's door for her. "Where are you going?"

"I rented a cabin at a mountain lake. I'll stay there until I hear from your parents. Your dad was coy about you guys. Where are you going? Why can't you come with me? And Thomas, where's your sister?"

Thomas froze and then glanced at Michael. His chin wobbled and he tightened his face.

Chris gave Aunt Sylvia a hug. "Don't worry 'bout us. We have a small errand to run."

Her forehead crinkled. "Well, I don't know what the big secret is all about."

Michael closed the trunk and walked to Aunt Sylvia. "We'll call you if we need help." He gave her a hug. Had she lost weight? It seemed she hadn't been well lately.

She slid into her seat and Chris closed the door. They watched her car until it disappeared behind the curve in the driveway.

"Where is Katherine?" Thomas asked. "How long can it take to climb a stupid mountain?"

Chris put his arm over Thomas's shoulders. "Dunno. I hope she calls soon. Robert could be here any time after three. We have to cut out before then."

Michael turned and walked towards the house. "Let's take the truck and get supplies. Oh, and we should buy a dinghy while were at it."

"Dinghy?" Thomas asked.

Michael turned to him and walked backwards. "Inflatable boat, with a motor. One of those valleys has a river and a lake, may as well prepare for it."

They jogged through the house and into the garage. Chris punched the button and opened the garage door. Michael strode around Chris to the driver's door and opened it.

Chris jumped in. "I'm driving." He grabbed the hold handle and pulled the door closed. Michael pulled it open again. "No way, I wanna."

Chris slammed the door closed. "First, I wanna too. I wanna live. Second, I've got my learner's."

Michael frowned and stomped to the passenger door, opened it and leaned in. "Yeah, but you'll lose it driving without an adult. I won't."

"Because you don't have one, Michael. Shut up and tell me where to go."

"I'll tell you where to go all right."

Michael stepped in and sat down. Thomas hopped into the back. Chris backed the truck out and crawled down the driveway. He was such a slow driver. Michael hated it.

"Here it is," Michael said. Chris pulled into the parking lot of Nick's Boating Warehouse and plowed through a minefield of potholes. Michael bounced off his seat and grabbed the hold handle. The parking lot was gravel and dotted with tufts of yellow spear grass. The building was built of cinder block, long since browned with rust and old paint. The metal roof was once green and the 'N' on the store sign was washed away. Chris pulled up to the front doors and stopped the truck. "Ick's Boating Warehouse," Chris said as he hopped out. "Place looks more like a salvage yard."

Michael opened his door and stepped from the truck. The place smelled like pee. "Grave yard, you mean."

Thomas dashed around the truck and sidled up beside Michael, pressing his shoulder into Michael's arm. Thomas's mouth was a thin line and his jaw hardened.

They pushed through the doors.

Michael's skin erupted into gooseflesh. The clerk's eyes were black and shone with malice. His hair was flattened with grease and his shoulders littered with dandruff. The man grinned. He was missing a front tooth and his fleshy tongue was pushed into the gaping hole. His tongue was easier to look at than the brown, crooked pegs surrounding it.

Michael lurched to a stop. Chris looked at him and raised his eyebrow. One thing Chris could do that Michael couldn't – a Spock eye.

"Geez," Michael whispered, "they left the place to a killer. God help us if he likes children."

"Shush," Chris said.

"How do they make money?" Thomas asked.

"Whad'ya you guys want?" The man yelled, spreading the 'you' like peanut butter.

Michael shivered. "Uh, an inflatable and a motor."

"You little dirps?" the man said. "Go away. You're wasting my time."

Chris stepped to the counter. "We've got money."

"Where'd you steal it from?" the man asked. He leaned onto the counter and stared into Michael's eyes. Michael felt sick.

"You're that kid. Yeah, I remember. Killed your mother, didn't you?"

Michael's mouth turned sour and he felt his face turn red. He slammed his fist onto the counter, hopped over it, threw himself onto the man, and knocked him to the floor. Michael punched him in the mouth and his fist stung as teeth grazed his skin off. Michael swung both fists into the man's face and blood spewed from the man's mouth, and his eyebrow split open. Michael punched him again, and again, and again.

Someone jumped on Michael's back, pressing his face into the man's hair. It stunk of rot.

"What the hell are you doing?" The man screamed.

Michael gagged at the stench of stale chew.

"Michael," Chris yelled, "get off him!"

Michael's arms were wrenched back, pulling him over. He jumped up and charged. Chris jumped on his back, knocking him down, and pinning him to the floor.

"You! You, get outta the store!" the man screamed. He stood, hunched like a chimpanzee, and wiped the blood off his mouth with his sleeve. "I'm gonna call the cops!"

"You didn't have to be such a jerk!" Chris yelled.

Michael felt tired. Chris pulled him to his feet, shoved him around the counter, and out through the door. Thomas was crying.

"It's all right, Thomas," Michael said.

Chris opened the truck door and pushed Michael inside. Michael placed his face into his hands. Thomas sniveled in the back seat.

"You all right, Thomas?" Michael asked.

Chris jumped into the truck. "That went well."

Michael started to shake. "I would have killed him."

"Don't be silly, Michael."

"No, I would have killed him if I had my knife."

"You need help then," Chris said.

"Yep, do," Michael said.

Chris backed up the truck. "Let's get some food. McDonalds?"

Thomas sniffed. "Sure, why not?"

Michael grabbed his seat belt and clipped it in. "I need to take a shower."

Chris turned the truck to the right. They blew out of the parking lot and onto the highway. The tires hummed against the tarred pavement. Michael opened his window and tilted his head back. The warm air blasted his hair into a frenzy. It felt good. He cranked up the radio. CJ98.5 -- old people's music, would keep Chris happy. Neil Diamond sung "I am, I Said" and Michael hummed along. Neil Diamond was an old guy but he had some good songs. Lost between two shores -- Michael could relate. But a frog that wanted to be king? Silly. He noticed his fists were clenched and he relaxed them. His knuckles stung and were bloody. He wiped them on his jeans. What if that rotting mouth infected his blood?

Chris slowed down and turned right. The road led to the lab their parents worked at. It was a huge compound full of buildings and surrounded by a massive brick fence. After the lab, they would follow a ninety-degree turn to the left at the hill, drive alongside the hill below their old neighborhood, and into town. They were close to their old home and Michael thought of the gopher snake. He grinned. He wished he could still do stuff like that and feel good about it.

Chris hunched over and looked into the rear view mirror. "Hey, guys. What's that? In the sky behind us?"

Michael hung out of his window and twisted back. "Hmm? Doesn't make sense." He pulled back into the truck, took off his seat belt, and turned onto his knees, looking through the back window. Thomas had done the same.

A black cloud filled the sky and it was rushing towards them. "Jeez, Chris. I don't know. Thomas?"

"I...I don't know, guys. Swarm of locusts?"

Michael stared, unblinking. "Speed up, Chris. I don't like the look of this. I think it's after us."

Michael was pressed into the seat back as the truck accelerated. The black cloud started to glitter. Shiny things swirled inside of it -- a whole bunch of them. "What are they? Propellers?" His skin tingled. "Helicopters! They're huge! Holy, there must be twenty of them."

"After us?" Chris said. "We can't be that important." The truck accelerated. "I'm really breaking the limit now," he said.

"Least of our problems," Michael said. "Can you count them, Thomas?"

"Already did. Sixteen, I think. It looks like a war movie. Are we being invaded?"

The helicopters were a few hundred feet behind them. Michael had never experienced a tornado, but he bet it sounded like this.

"It looks military," Thomas yelled. "I think they're full of soldiers."

The truck started to lift and weave.

"Chris, stop. It's too dangerous," Michael yelled.

Chris swung the truck onto the shoulder and yelled something at Michael, but he couldn't hear. The helicopters were right above them. Michael leaned out of his window and looked up. The down draft pushed his eyelids closed and he had to concentrate to see. The choppers were black and seemed too large to be in the air. They blasted by and down the road.

Chris's mouth dropped open. "What the? Where are they going?"

Michael felt the blood rush from his face. "The lab! The machine. Freakin' Robert. He's going after the machine!"

"How do you know?" Thomas asked.

Michael turned to look at him. Thomas's eyes were bugged out. "What else could it be? It just makes sense."

"Put your belts on," Chris said. He popped the truck into drive and screeched onto the highway. "I have a lookout above the compound."

Chris topped ninety miles an hour. The fence surrounding the lab compound was visible. It was brick, twelve feet high and topped with broken glass. Michael used to sit against it and wait, hoping to catch his parents leaving through the front gate.

The two biggest helicopters flew to the tallest building in the compound, the one their parents worked in, and hovered above it. The rest dropped behind the fence.

Chris reached the southern edge of the fence. Michael stared into the brick wall as they zoomed by, wishing he had x-ray vision. The compound gate whipped by but so fast he couldn't see inside. They sped to the far corner at the bottom of the hill and Chris slammed on the brakes, laying a patch of rubber down the pavement. He threw open the door and jumped out. "Grab the binoculars from the glove box, Michael. Follow me." He dashed around the brick wall and disappeared. Thomas jumped out and ran after him.

Michael grabbed the binoculars and jumped from the truck as Thomas disappeared around the corner. Michael followed him, around the wall onto a dirt path, into the birch forest, and up the hill.

Thomas, about thirty feet ahead, cut right and disappeared. Michael ran to the spot and veered into a patch of bushes. Where was Chris taking them? He broke into a grassy clearing with a rock in the middle. It was flat, two-feet high, and the size of a trampoline. Chris and Thomas were standing on it, staring down at the compound. Michael jumped onto the rock and ran to them.

"Hurry," Chris said, "the binoculars."

They were perched at the top of a cliff, about eighty feet higher than the compound. The compound was swarming with soldiers dressed in black, each carrying a submachine gun. One of the choppers, a carrier, hovered over the skylight of their parents' building, a three story brick building at the far end of the compound.

"The chopper dropped a platform into the skylight," Chris said. "Smashed it."

Machine gun fire rattled through the compound. "Lab security," Chris said. "They took out three of them. There must be a hundred soldiers in there."

"Army?" Michael asked. "You think they're military? Black uniforms?"

"Don't know. Soldiers of some kind."

Michael felt weak, and he sat down. This was insane. Was it an invasion? Were they at war? He glanced down the road looking for the army, but there wasn't a vehicle in sight.

The door of the lab building flew open and a stream of soldiers ran out. They scattered to the helicopters and hopped in. The lifter rose with the platform under it, and with a rectangular object, wrapped in a tarp, on the platform. The helicopters rose and zipped away in different directions. The lifter flew north, towards their house.

It grew quiet and the sound of crickets filled the air. A dog barked somewhere above.

Chris lowered the binoculars. "No way. No way. Who can do something like that?"

"The government," Michael said. "The UN. We've gotta find out what that machine is."

"Energy," Thomas said. "It's gotta be a new form of energy."

Michael stood. His legs felt like chewing gum. "But it needs energy to run it. The turbine?"

Chris stood up. "Come on. We have to focus on Katherine. Let's get home."

CHAPTER 21

Katherine was mesmerized by the mountain lion's eyes. They were pale green and ringed by a black circle of fur, like a Goth with heavy eyeliner, and exuded a mysterious and hypnotic force. It was magical.

She marveled at the power and beauty of the creature. It must have weighed more than one hundred and fifty pounds, fifty more than she did. Its jaws could wrap around her head. Its tail was four feet long and each paw was as large as a rabbit. Muscles rippled under its fur coat with every twitch. Its nose was black and its nostrils were ringed with the color of autumn leaves.

A dragonfly flopped onto her gun.

"Seriously?" She blinked and shook it off.

The mountain lion twitched its whiskers, raised its head, and sniffed her. It parted its mouth, revealing a massive pink tongue. Its teeth were huge and glistened with saliva. A vampire would be envious.

It tensed its legs in a motion almost imperceptible. Katherine squeezed the trigger. She would have one shot. If she missed, she'd die.

It was such a beautiful animal. She hoped she wouldn't be forced to take its life.

It sprang, leapt across the river, and landed eight feet in front of her. Katherine screamed and dropped the gun. It rattled down the rocks, flipped up, and flew towards the mountain lion. The creature sprang straight up, like a kitten attacking a ball of wool, turned in mid-air, and hit the ground running. It disappeared into the forest.

"Right choice, buddy."

Her knees gave out and she fell; she laid her head on the ground and cried.

"God, I can't do this. Please help." Her scabs were cracking in the heat and oozing pus. Her bruises ached. Her muscles were wound up and her fingers hurt when she moved them. Her senses were in high gear -- every noise seemed louder and her vision was as sharp as a tack. She had moved from humanity to raw survival, and it was exhausting.

She wiped the tears off her cheeks and stood up. She staggered to the gun, picked it up, and placed it into the holster. She picked up the water bottle, added a few drops of iodine, screwed on the cap, and bundled up her possessions. She turned and looked up. Her stomach growled.

She had five hundred feet of scree to climb and then a few hundred feet of boulders, each the size of a playhouse. Sometime in the past they had fallen from the mountain face, leaving a cliff about a hundred feet high. How would she climb that?

She recalled the playhouse and smiled. She'd been five years old. The playhouse was being raffled off at the Northwood Mall. It had had two stories, a front door that had just brushed the top of her head when she walked in, and had been pink with white trim. She'd thought it was Barbie's house and she'd wanted it so badly that she'd cried when they'd left the mall. Her mom hadn't been able to afford the five-dollar raffle ticket. Katherine had been sure she'd have won it. She'd been so mad at her mom.

She shrugged, and plowed her foot into the dusty rock shards.

Katherine stopped and checked the time. An hour had passed. She turned and looked down the avalanche of shale, as long as a football field and steeper than a black diamond ski run. A wind gust pushed her forward and her head spun. She fell onto her back, blowing a dust cloud into the air. She shook her hair and ran her fingers through it. It was brittle and dirty, and she hated that. She longed for a shower. She coughed and sneezed. The air felt thin.

The valley was sprawled beneath her. The hundred-foot trees looked like pencils. The crash site was a blemish, for the most part hidden by the foliage surrounding it. She couldn't see over the mountains lining the west side of the valley, and would have to climb to the peak to get high enough.

She turned over and leaned into the mountain to hold her balance. She had twenty feet of scree to climb to reach the rock belt.

She took a step and slid back, setting off an avalanche of shale. She clawed at the rocks and looked for something to grab onto. A gnarled pine tree rose from the soil six feet ahead. She thrust the walking stick into the rocks and leapt towards it. She grabbed the tree and pulled herself up. *Good. Almost there.*

She scrambled up another six feet, grabbed and held onto a bunch of grass, and lay down and panted. *One more.* She stood up, took a deep breath and ran towards the closest boulder. She started to slide backwards. She drove her legs harder and pushed forward, grabbing the boulder and pulling herself around to its side. She sat down and rested. She was inside a crevice between two boulders, just wider than her shoulders. It was cool and dark, and the blue sky illuminated the jagged rocks around her. She stepped on a shelf in the boulder to her left and then onto an impression in the boulder to her right, and climbed up between them. She pulled herself onto the top.

The boulders created an unusually flat surface, considering an avalanche had created them. She hopped onto the next boulder, sprinted across, and leapt a crevice to another one. She grinned. This would be fun, she thought.

Katherine sat on the ground at the base of the cliff and threw her arms in the air. "Yes!" The rock belt lay below her.

A cool breeze whipped around the cliff base. It felt nice.

Her white socks lay bare through slices in her canvas Nike shoes, shredded by the shale. The sole of the left shoe was separated at the toe. "They'll have to do," she said as she dragged herself off the ground.

Katherine turned and stared up the cliff. A fall from thirty feet would kill her, let alone one hundred. She scanned the cliff to her right and then to her left. Further down the cliff broke into small plateaus, like rice paddies carved into a Chinese mountainside. The vertical climb between each plateau looked about thirty feet, sometimes more. A fall would break bones, but maybe not kill her.

"Great," she lamented while walking towards the spot.

She dropped the walking stick, pulled out the water bottle and gulped some water down. It was warm like the water the dentist rinsed her teeth with. She placed the bottle on the ground beside the shirt and its contents to pick up on her return.

She grabbed a ledge cut into the cliff, lifted her foot and put it back down. She looked down at the stick, picked it up, placed it against her knee and pulled, breaking off a one-foot piece. She jammed the piece into the back of her pants, broke off another, shoved it in beside the first, and tucked the shirt over them.

She walked to the cliff, stood back, and scanned the face looking for hand holds. Butterflies invaded her stomach.

"Pixie dust. I need Pixie dust."

Ledges were cut through the cliff side, many just big enough for her fingertips. She reached over her head, grabbed the first outcrop, and hooked the fingers of her right hand over it. She pulled down. It held. She lifted her right foot and placed it on a small ledge of moss about the width of her big toe. Taking a breath, she lunged up. The ledges held, but she swung away. Gasping, she pulled in and clawed at the cliff with her left hand. She caught a small vertical crack. She drove her hand into the crack and pushed her knuckles out to create a wedge, scraping the scabs off her skin.

"Keep going, Katherine. Don't look down."

She drew up her left foot and wedged it between the crack. She looked up and targeted a small outcropping for her right hand. She lunged up and grabbed it with three fingers. She clawed the cliff with her right foot and found a resting place.

"Great, Katherine. Two steps." She reached up for the next outcropping and thought about her brother. What was he doing right now? Had they gotten him? He was such a cute little fart, with mousy hair, a fine nose, and a pout hard not to fall for. Girls would go nuts over him if he had some confidence to go with it.

She pushed herself up and hooked her right fingers into a ledge high above her head. She shoved her right foot into a crack and, hugging the cliff with her shaking body, elevated herself another two feet.

She hoped Robert Cain hadn't gone for Thomas. She was overwhelmed by a surge of anger, and clenched her teeth. If someone had laid a finger on Thomas, she'd hunt him down and kill him.

She looked up and was surprised to find herself near the first plateau.

"Come on, Katherine, you can do it." She swung her right arm over the plateau above her head and clawed at the ground. Her left hand, placed just above her waist, started to slip. She swung away from the cliff. Panic fired adrenalin to every nerve in her body. She was going to fall. Something brushed her right hand index finger. She sprung up and grabbed it. It felt like a tree root. She pushed hard with her legs, pulled herself over, and collapsed onto her back.

Her fingernails were packed with dirt, and they hurt.

She shaded her eyes with her arm. The clouds were so close she felt she could reach up and touch them. They were thin and wispy, like bridal veils. She thought of Christopher. She was about to break up with him and now she needed him more than ever. "Get up, Katherine."

She sat up and looked into the valley. The trees were tiny, like the moss etching an existence into the rock under her feet. She couldn't see the crash site. The mountains on the other side of the valley loomed up in front of her, blocking her view to the outside. They were slightly shorter than the mountain she was climbing. She had to reach the peak to see over them.

She turned to the cliff and looked up to the next obstacle. This one was thirty feet high. A V-shaped crevice about the width of her body ran up the right side of it. It was almost vertical, but not quite. The V was sprinkled with crevices and foot holds. With a burst of energy she stood up and grabbed an outcropping, placed her foot onto a ledge, pushed herself up, and reached with her right hand, hooking her fingers over a crevice. She had climbed walls back home but they didn't come close to this.

Pushing herself up, she remembered her dad's voice, and she shuddered. He was screaming at her. He stunk of rum and his eyes were wild. "Where's Thomas?" he'd yelled while poking his finger into her shoulder.

She pushed up and grabbed the next ledge, and found a spot for her right foot. She could sense when Dad was crazed the moment he'd closed the garage door. She'd jump out of bed, wake up Thomas, and push him into the cellar under the stairs. God, he'd been so scared. She had never told her dad where she'd hidden Thomas and it had infuriated him.

She reached up and grabbed an outcropping with her left hand. It crumbled and her foot slipped. She looked down, twenty-five feet to fall. Her arms were shaking, and she wanted to give up, to jump. But what if she didn't die? She saw herself lying on the rock shelf below, paralyzed with a broken back, covered with snow and an eagle plucking her eyeball out. She clawed at the cliff with her left hand and her fingers held. Panting, she reached up again, found a crack in the cliff, jammed her fingers into it, and pushed up.

Dad had pulled off his belt and she had started to tremble. Where was Mom? She had sensed her mom. She had felt her mom's fear. Why had Mom hidden when Dad had done this to her?

Katherine hauled herself onto the second ledge and turned to the last cliff. Without looking up, she placed her foot on an outcropping the height of her knee, and grabbed a scraggly bush growing from the cliff. Her muscles stung like the belt whipping her skin, across her legs, back, and arms. She tried to shake the memories, but couldn't. She reached for the next handhold, grabbed it, and pushed herself up. She could smell rum from her memories and needed to vomit.

She'd refused to cry out when her dad had belted her. She wouldn't have given him the satisfaction.

She felt the sting of his belt again, and jumped up and grabbed the next ledge.

He had shown no expression when he'd belted her. When he'd gotten tired, he'd thrown the belt down and had started to punch. She'd covered her head with her arms and had fallen to her knees, which had angered him even more.

She receded inwards, not thinking beyond the next ledge, crevice, or foothold. She forced her dad from her mind and saw Thomas.

She'd had held Thomas and they'd quivered under the stairs. Their dad had turned on their mom then. They had often heard her screaming upstairs. Thomas had been so frail, so scared. Katherine had often sung to him and he had whimpered. The bruises had started to show and she had tried to hide them from him.

She reached up and felt a crack in the rock, and jammed her hand into it. She started to cry and the tears blurred her vision. She hardly ever cried, until today. She shook and sobbed, and almost slipped. She brought her right foot up, but she couldn't see and scraped her toe down the cliff-side. Tears flowed down her cheeks. She felt dizzy, and sick, and the bruises and welts covering her body started to throb. She pushed herself up, wiped her eyes with her sleeve, and reached over the top. She ran her fingertips over the cold rock and found a ridge just big enough for her fingertips. She curled her fingers into it and leapt up while kicking her feet into the cliff. She pulled up onto her forearms. The weight of her legs pulled her back down. She screamed and threw her right leg over and rolled away from the edge. Laying her face onto the snow, she quivered and cried.

She saw her dad again, and she saw herself jump up and punch him in the chest. He looked surprised and she swung at him again. He fell to his knees and put his hands above his head. She screamed in anger and swung her fists onto his head.

She realized she was pounding the snow. It was cold.

Katherine had no idea how long she'd been crying. Her chest and stomach hurt and she was exhausted. She felt empty, empty of the poison she'd pent up over the years. It was a lonely feeling, like a discarded pop can in a filthy alley, but it felt good too.

She sat up, looked down the cliff and threw her fist into the air. "You son of a bitch!"

She sighed. *Come on, Katherine. Get it together.*

She was sitting at the edge of a snow filled plateau about the size of a football field. The mountain peak rose above it. A bowl shaped lake, twenty feet in diameter and filled with emerald water, lay in the middle of the plateau. She remembered the green angel in her coffin, and her body grew warm. A ridge rose up to her left, at the edge of the plateau, ramping two hundred feet, the height of a twenty-story building, where it met a cliff-top. On top of the cliff was a ninety-foot snow cap, ramping near vertically to the peak. The snowcap flowed down the peak and reached over the cliff edge, like a frozen wave, for a full thirty feet, to a one hundred-foot plummet into the lake.

The sun's rays filled the bowl with glittering diamonds and she squinted. She tore a sleeve off her shirt, cut a slit into it for each eye, placed it over her eyes, and tied it behind her head.

Katherine walked to the lake, filled her hands, and drank. The water froze her throat and stomach, but it felt great.

"Get going, Katherine, or you'll freeze to death."

She stumbled to the ridge. It was like a staircase, about three feet across. It grew steeper as it rose. On her left was a sheer one thousand-foot cliff. She gasped and staggered back. She took a deep breath, another, and stepped onto the ledge, starting her final ascent.

Katherine had climbed the ramp in only ten minutes. It was easier than she'd expected. She stepped off, placing her foot onto the snow pack. Her foot slipped and she fell, slamming her shoulder into the ice.

"Ouch."

She pushed off the snow, back to the rock ledge, and looked up. She shuddered. How could she reach the peak climbing a skating rink?

She pulled one of the sticks from her waist and jammed it into the snow. It cracked through the surface, blowing chunks of ice into the air. She watched them slide down the peak and fly off the end. She counted. "1, 2, 3, 4, 5, 6." The splash was faint.

She grabbed the stick and pulled herself onto the snow pack. It held.

She plowed the next stick in, reached up, and pulled herself to it. She pulled out the first stick and jammed her foot in the hole.

Her lungs burned. In spite of the cold temperature, blowing snow, and meager clothing, sweat dripped from her brow. She was panting and her arms shook. She kicked in a foothold, pulled out the stick and pushed up another four feet.

She counted her forty-fifth step as she crawled onto the peak. She was drenched in sweat and shivering. She stood, keeping her knees bent, storing energy needed to fight the wind.

"Beautiful." She was surrounded with snow-capped peaks and valleys, like ocean waves, for as far as she could see. Her heart sunk. "Middle of nowhere."

She leaned over as far as she dared and looked down the peakside. The vertical drop threw off her balance and made her dizzy. She fell to her knees and sat on her feet. "Where the heck am I?"

She scanned the jumble of peaks, trying to find a landmark. She could see nothing discernible to the east or south. She turned west.

Her heart pounded and she smiled.

"Ah-hah! Got it."

She looked north. "Even better."

Katherine pulled the phone out of her pocket and flipped it open. She gasped. No service.

"Why are you testing me like this!" She stood up and held the phone high above her head. She rotated and watched the service indicator. A tiny blip appeared, just one indicator bar out of a possible five. She typed out her message, held the phone up high, and pressed send.

She crouched into a ball and waited. Her teeth chattered. Two minutes passed and she hadn't received a failure message.

She looked down the slope, a ninety-foot Olympic ski jump, and shuddered. If she fell she'd fly off the end of it and plunge one hundred feet into the lake below. She envisioned a full, double, full, full, and a layout as she hit the water and grinned. "Still got your sense of humor." She sighed.

The blowing snow had buried her footprints. She turned around, faced the peak, and placed her hands down to a bear-walk. She grabbed a stick from her jeans and raised it high above her ahead as though preparing to drive a stake through the heart of a vampire. Grunting, she drove the stick down. It struck the ice, shattered, and flew out of her hand. The pieces slid down the snowcap, picking up speed as they went, and rocketed over the edge.

"Great," she said. "An omen."

She gripped the last stick so tightly her knuckles were white. She raised it high and drove it into the snow. It shattered through the ice and anchored. She grabbed onto the stick and lowered herself down. She kicked the crust with her right foot once, twice, three times. Her foot broke through.

She lowered herself and kicked the ice with her left foot until it broke through. She grabbed the stick and pulled hard. It popped out of the ground and she screamed, fell over onto her back, and started to slide. Ice crystals jumped around her like a ring of fire, and she rocketed down.

She pushed her elbow into the snow, flipped onto her back, and kicked her heels into the ice. It wouldn't give. The snow crystals were blasting into her face and she couldn't see how far it was before she'd fly off the end.

She flipped onto her stomach, grabbed the stick with both hands and jammed it into the snow, but she kept sliding. She wrapped her right arm around the stick and grasped the top of it with her left. She screamed like a sensei cracking through a stack of boards and pushed all her weight onto the stick. It jumped and buckled and scratched the surface. She pushed harder. It dug in, ever so slightly. She pushed harder and started to slow.

Her feet shot into the air. She screamed in remorse for, once again, she was about to die. She shut her eyes, waiting for the plummet, for her stomach to get sucked down to the core of her body, for the dizzying drop. She wondered if she would feel pain when hitting the rocks under the lake.

Her legs flew up and crashed down, and hung over the esker.

The stick held.

She banged her forehead into the snow and screamed with fury. Her muscles cramped. The snow burned her stomach. Her arm trembled out of control. She couldn't hang on.

"Katherine!" She sobbed. "You can do it!"

A small voice whispered in her head. "It's okay, Katherine. It's okay."

She saw herself as a child, running through a field of yellow daisies. She was wearing her favorite blue skirt. She saw a bunny rabbit in the flowers and she wanted to catch it. She wanted it to be her pet.

"No, Katherine!" She screamed. "Ignore them. It's not all right! You can do this!"

Or was it all right? What if she just let go? She was so tired. She couldn't do it. She couldn't pull herself up. She couldn't even hold on anymore.

"This little light of mine, I'm gonna let it shine. This little light of mine, I'm gonna let it shine. Thomas, I love you. I'm sorry I can't be there for you anymore"

She relaxed her grip. Her fingers slipped. All went black.

CHAPTER 22

Michael grabbed the remote from the table and switched to the security cameras, filling the wall with views from the barn, the yard, and the house. They had been watching news reports of the lab break-in for the past hour and Michael was getting sick of it. He hated TV news anchors. They were parrots, squawking the same stuff. They didn't have a clue.

They showed a couple of employee cell phone videos of the attack at first, but weren't showing them anymore. There were theories as to who had done it, but the only thing they agreed on was that the caper was huge and well beyond the abilities of even the mafia.

Chris tossed a pepperoni pizza on the table and grabbed a piece.

Thomas sat and stared at the screen.

"Where is she?" Michael said. "Two-thirty's cutting it way too close..."

"Oh girl you make me feel like whoa, spinning me..."

Thomas jumped up. "Yes!"

Chris snatched the phone from the table.

"What did she say?" Thomas asked.

"Couple of things. Huge mountain long ways away South West. More West. End of valley curls and points right to it. Lake North of valley. River runs from it and through. Mountain peaks all over."

Michael ran to the computer and pulled up Google Earth.

"Get me your maps, Thomas."

Michael called up the first location. Chris and Thomas were leaning on his shoulders. He locked his toes onto the desk legs to stop them from pushing him out of his seat.

"The valleys run straight north to south," Chris said.

"And there's no lake," Thomas said.

"Nope, next one." Michael grabbed the second map from Thomas. He punched in the co-ordinates and they waited breathless while Google Earth zoomed into it.

"Shoot," Chris said, "no river."

"Third time lucky," Michael said. Thomas passed him the third map. The valley had a river. "Looking good."

Michael punched in the coordinates and his heart started to pound. "Has a lake on top. With Google Earth, he flew south down the valley, over the river and to the end. He raised the view above the mountain range and gasped. "That mountain is huge." He clicked on it.

"Baker. Mount Baker," Thomas squealed.

"This has gotta be it, "Michael said. "Chilcolten Lake to the north. Chilcolten River runs through it, the valley points to Mount Baker, and it's at a twenty-one hundred foot elevation."

"Geez," Chris said. "I hope Katherine didn't climb one of those peaks."

"Yeah, they look flippin' dangerous," Michael said. He panned over the top of one. "Cinder Mountain." He felt weak. "Holy, sixty-three hundred feet. She would have to climb forty-two hundred feet to reach the top of it."

"She wouldn't have gone to the top, would she?" Thomas whispered.

"Let's see," Michael said. He moved beside the mountain and panned west. "Can't see over the other side from here. He flew up the side of the mountain while staring across the valley. "Wow, guys, you can't see Mount Baker until you're on top of this thing."

"Jeez," Thomas said, "how's she gonna get down?"

"Same way she got up," Michael said, "only faster. Look how close Chilcolten Lake is. It has a campground and everything. She could hike out in an hour if she had to."

Chris patted Michael's shoulder. "Good job, Michael. I'll send her a text. If we don't get to her by tomorrow night she should hike out to the lake."

Michael stood up. "Let's go. Chilcolten is a four-hour drive. We should be there by dinner."

Movement caught Michael's eye. He glanced at the screen. "Shoot!"

Chris looked up from his phone. "What?"

"Red Escalade just pulled into the driveway."

"Great," Chris said, "now what?"

Thomas walked in front of the screen. "Robert?"

Michael's heart pounded. "Probably. Oh shoot!" He jumped out of his chair. "The ladder!" He raced to the door and threw it open, dashed to the ladder, dragged it up, and tossed it on the ground by the wall.

Chris appeared beside him and looked over the mezzanine. "Geez, look at the footprints down there. It'll be obvious we're up here."

"Nothin' we can do about it. Grab these bails," Michael said. He laced his fingers through a bailing string and dragged a block of hay to the platform edge, placing it over their path. Chris pulled one up behind him.

Thomas grabbed a bale and pulled it across. "Hurry guys, they could be outside the barn right now."

"Put that one beside Chris's," Michael said.

Chris grabbed another bale and tossed it on top of Thomas's. "That should do it."

"Shush," Thomas whispered.

Two men were talking outside the barn. One laughed. "Get inside," Michael whispered. He let Chris and Thomas by, followed them into their headquarters, and closed the door.

Thomas and Chris were staring at the screen. "They're here," Thomas whispered.

The hoodie guy squeezed through the doors. A man sauntered up behind him.

"The hoodie guy, Sith," Chris said. "I thought he died at the island."

"Sith?" Thomas asked.

"He works for Robert," Michael said. "We call him Sith. His name's Bill."

Michael thought back to their community playground where Bill had smoked cigarettes and watched for them. He had always worn sunglasses, covered his head with a hoodie, and smoked. Chris had nicknamed him Sith because he had reminded him of Darth Maul.

The men walked to the middle of the barn and stopped. Bill stared into the camera.

"Scary looking," Thomas said.

Bill pointed to the right side of the barn. "Check the right side, Brandon. I'll take the left." He paced along the barn wall and peered around the tractor and into the horse stalls.

"Ever heard of Brandon?" Michael asked.

"Nope," Chris said.

"What are we looking for?" Brandon asked.

"Don't know for sure. From what I know of these little brats, they're good at hiding. I wonder if there's a false wall behind that hay up there?"

"Where?"

Bill pointed at the platform. "Up there."

"Only one way to find out," Brandon said.

"Yeah," Bill said, "go get it."

"Huh?" Michael said.

Brandon left the barn.

"What are they up to?" Chris said.

Brandon walked to the Escalade, popped open the back, and pulled out a red Jerry Jug.

"No, they wouldn't," Michael whispered.

Brandon slipped into the barn and walked towards them, and disappeared under the mezzanine.

"I should have placed a camera from the other direction," Michael said.

"That's not gasoline is it?" Thomas said.

"Sure looks like it," Chris said.

"Shush," Michael said. He held his breath, trying to hear what Brandon was doing. There was a muffled roar outside. "What the heck is that?"

Magnified by the camera, smoke billowed up the wide screen TV.

"Fire!" Michael yelled.

"Get outta here!" Chris screamed.

"Don't panic," Michael said. "Grab your laptops."

Michael tore his laptop plug out of the wall and placed it in the bag. The server fans sucked the smoke from under the raised floor and blew it into the room. It stung Michael's throat and he coughed.

"Chris?"

"Over here," Chris said. "By the refrigerator."

"Both of you?"

"Uh-huh."

Michael pressed his mouth to his sleeve and staggered towards Chris's voice. He ran into the table, pushed it aside, and bumped into Chris.

"Hold onto my shirt, Chris. Thomas, you hold Chris's shirt."

"And let you guide us to our deaths?" Thomas yelled.

"No time for jokes, Thomas." Michael dropped to his knees and crawled, sweeping his hand past the fridge and onto the wall. He felt his way past the screen.

Couple more feet.

Michael felt a ring in the floor. He pulled on it and opened a hatch.

"We have to hurry guys. The escape is filled with smoke."

Michael stepped in, grabbed a rail, and stumbled down a narrow flight of stairs.

Landing on solid ground, he groped the wall on his left, turned a lever, and threw open a half door. He dropped to the ground and crawled out. Chris and Thomas fell beside him. They crawled through the grass for twenty feet, up to the forest edge, and looked back at the barn.

Flames roared through the barn roof and one of the windows shattered. "Jerks!"

"We have to get to the truck," Chris said.

"You go first, Chris. Get the truck out of the garage. We'll meet you outside."

Chris ducked down and leapt into the forest. Flames burst through the fire escape door.

"Thomas, let's go!"

Thomas didn't budge. He was crying.

"Come on!" Michael grabbed Thomas's hand and pulled him into the forest.

"Stay low, Thomas. We're heading to the shop."

Michael crouched and raced through the trees, staying close to the edge. He circled the yard to the riverside cliff-top and ran towards the shop.

"I can see them," Thomas yelled.

The barn groaned. The south wall collapsed and the roof crashed down. Bill and Brandon stood by the Escalade, looking at the fire with their hands on their hips.

"I hope the cat got out," Michael said. "Follow me, to the shed."

They broke from the trees and dashed to the shed, dropping down behind the north wall.

"I think they saw us," Thomas said.

"They looked our way?"

"Yeah, I think so."

"Let's wait," Michael said. "One, two, three, four, five, six, seven, eight, go!"

Michael jumped up, ran alongside the north shop wall, and careened around the corner of the building.

"Gah!" Michael slid to a stop.

Bill stood twenty feet away by the southwest corner of the building. He raised a handgun and pointed it at Michael. "Unfinished business." He smiled.

Michael glanced behind him. *Where is Thomas?*

A hoe swung from around the corner of the workshop and smashed into Bill's head. His eyes rolled back and he collapsed. Thomas stepped out and over Bill and dropped the hoe onto the ground.

"Where did you come from?" Michael asked.

"Other side of the shed."

"What is it with you and hoes?"

"Practice makes perfect," Thomas said. "Picked the right side this time."

Something whistled by Michael's head and thunked into the tree behind him, and the crack of a gunshot echoed through the air.

"Brandon," Thomas yelled, "he's shooting!"

"Run!" Michael yelled. He pushed Thomas towards the house. "Around the back."

A birch tree splintered beside Thomas's head.

They sprinted along the trees, behind the house, and around the garage. Chris was waiting in the truck. "Jump in!" he yelled.

A bullet hit the passenger door with a bang.

"Stay down!" Michael yelled. He threw open the back door, grabbed Thomas by his pants, and tossed him in. He jumped onto Thomas and slammed the door as Chris stomped on the gas, screeching the tires over the asphalt. Chris cranked the steering wheel and flipped the truck around, popped it into drive and screeched down the lane in a cloud of smoke.

"You guys all right?" Chris asked.

"Yep," Michael said.

"Get off me," Thomas wheezed.

Michael pushed off of Thomas and crawled over the centre console and into the front passenger seat. "Nice drift, Chris. It's almost like you know how to drive now. You should have seen Thomas. He whacked a hoe into Bill's head."

"Really?" Chris said.

"Yeah, Bill pulled a gun on me."

Chris turned the truck onto the highway. "Off to Chilcolten. There's no way Robert'll find us there. You don't suppose they know where the plane crashed, do you?"

Thomas poked his head up front. "Never thought of that. Do you think?"

A fire truck screamed past them.

"Don't know," Chris said. "Planes usually have homing beacons when they crash."

"I doubt this jet would have one," Michael said. "Robert wouldn't want it traced."

Thomas plunked back into his seat. "I hope Katherine's all right."

"I'm sure she's fine," Chris said.

They drove for half an hour, leaving the pine trees behind to sagebrush and cactus.

"How long can she live without food?" Thomas asked.

Michael turned to him. "With water, a couple of weeks. And she's got shelter. She's probably lying around waiting to be rescued."

Thomas's eyes seemed to turn dark. "What if her phone's out of batteries?"

"No problem. I've got her pinned. There's a hiking trail along the river. We can zip along it at a good pace. I'm guessing she's in one of the few places where the trail breaks from the river. It might take us a few hours, but I'm sure we'll have no problems finding her."

Thomas straightened up. "Are we hiking in tonight?"

"Probably. If it's really late we could stay at a hotel and leave in the morning."

"How would we pay, Michael? I doubt they'll take cash from a kid," Chris said.

"I'll pay over the net."

"With what?" Chris said.

"We're multi-millionaires. Remember?"

"Oh, right. Forgot."

They were driving through mountains on a four-lane highway. Michael stared into the trees rushing by, trying to push Bill's gun muzzle from his mind. His flesh tingled. His fists were clenched and his hands were shaking. He pushed them between his legs so Chris wouldn't notice. His legs started to shake. His chest started to shake. His lip quivered. He gritted his teeth and covered his face with his hands.

"Michael?" Chris asked.

"I...I." Michael was smothered in a deep sadness. It sucked the emotions from every part of his body into a cavern at the pit of his stomach. Tears streamed from his eyes.

Chris pulled the truck over and stopped. "Michael?"

"What is it?" Thomas asked.

Michael couldn't hold back. His face felt hot, tears dropped from his cheeks, he buried his head in his hands, folded over, and bawled.

Thomas popped over the console. "What's the matter with him?"

"Last time a gun was pointed at him we weren't so lucky," Chris said.

Michael felt Thomas's hand on his shoulder, and he was hit with a wave of guilt.

"I'm sorry, Thomas. I'm sorry I was so mean to you. I'm sorry I've gotten us into this mess."

"We're real close now," Thomas said. "We'll get her back."

CHAPTER 23

Wind buffeting a sail, it was one of the most beautiful sounds Katherine had ever heard, for the wind was lonely in its howling and the sail angry in its flapping, but they danced. While on sailing trips with her friend, Katherine would lay on the sailboat deck, close her eyes, and feel the sounds.

Dead people can't hear, so how can I hear the wind?

Consciousness ascended through Katherine and she became aware; she couldn't feel her feet; her hands were curled into monkey claws; her eyelids were glued shut; her body was frozen to the core.

Panic rose from her gut and she tried to scream, but only a single sob came out.

She lifted her hand, placed the back of it over her right eye, and felt balls of ice clinging to her lashes. The ice melted and the water ran down her sleeve, and when it stopped she moved her hand to her left eye.

She opened her eyes to a tornado of gold dust, swirling snow crystals reflecting the suns rays, and wondered if she was in heaven. But heaven couldn't possibly be this cold, could it?

She was in agony. Her stomach seared as though she lay on a frying pan and her calf muscles were curled into balls.

She raised her head, but she was stopped short by her hair. "What the...?"

She closed her eyes, gritted her teeth, and yanked her head up, tearing her hair from the ice. She squealed at the pain streaking through her skull and opened her eyes to a patch of hair stuck in the ice, circling down and through it like blood rich capillaries.

She looked up and her heart pounded. The stick, anchored into the snow, was a few feet above her head. She was still on the peak edge. *How?*

She reached up, wrapped her frozen hands around the stick, and pulled. She didn't move.

She placed her elbows into the snow and lifted her chest, and her shirt peeled from the ice like Velcro.

Sweat. I'm frozen to the ice.

She grabbed the stick again, pulled her right leg up from the precipice, and then her left. She pushed her knees under her chest and sat up. Snow fell from her back like salt from a saltshaker. She heaved on the stick and walked on her knees, pushing herself forward.

"Now what?"

She pushed her right hand into her pocket and felt the knife. She grabbed it and pulled. The cell phone flew out with the knife and flipped into the air. She dropped the knife and grabbed the phone but her fingers wouldn't close! The phone slipped from her palm and flew over the edge. The knife followed.

"Shoot!" She shook her head and swallowed the urge to cry.

She unclipped the gun holster, pulled the gun out, and slammed the barrel into the snow above the stick. It shattered through and lodged. The barrel was short and would pop out if she pulled at the wrong angle. And she couldn't grip with her frozen fingers. She wrapped her right hand around it.

"One, two, three."

She closed her eyes and let go of the stick. The gun held. Pulling against the gun she knee-walked to it, reached back, grabbed the stick, slammed it through the snow in front of her and pulled herself up. The ridge, leading from the snow peak and down to the lake, was to her left. She pulled the gun from the ice and pounded it back in, to her left. She traversed sideways across the peak like a crab. Snow crab, she thought. Reaching the ramp, she shuffled her legs onto it, and pushed herself off the peak.

She stood, her knees buckled, and she fell to the jagged rocks. She sat up, pushed her legs out straight, and leaned forward into a stretch. She bobbed, but she couldn't reach past her knees. She drew her legs up and down and wiggled her toes until some warmth came back, and mindful of the 1000-foot drop to her right, stood and stepped forward.

Her leg felt detached, like a prosthetic. She stepped down, not feeling her foot, and swung her left leg forward, while scanning the ground for a place to put it. Her foot landed on a rock and she stumbled towards the precipice, and threw herself down on to the ground just before plummeting over.

Katherine pushed herself up and picked out a path through the crevices and ridges lain in front of her, relaxed, and wove her way down. Her legs warmed and her feet tingled and started to hurt. She ran her fingers through her scalp and found the bald spot. It was about three fingers in width. She frowned. *I must look like a freak.*

She stepped off the ramp, staggered to the lake and looked into it. The water's surface was rippled and she sighed. She didn't want to see her reflection anyway.

Her body felt like sides of beef in cold storage. She needed to light a fire, but she had left the matches at the base of the cliff.

She reached into the water and splashed some on her face, and felt nothing.

She shuffled to the cliff, turned to face it, grabbed an outcrop and, lying on her stomach, pushed her legs over. She clawed with the tips of her toes until she found a ledge to rest them on, reached down with her right hand, blindly found a ridge, grasped it, and let go with her left. She forced herself to look down. She scanned the rock for a handhold and finding one grabbed onto it and lowered herself down. Climbing down was harder than climbing up, but faster. She was close to hypothermia and death. This was something she had to do to survive.

CHAPTER 24

The truck shuddered.
"Michael jolted awake. "Whah?"
"Rumble strips," Chris said.
Michael twisted his neck. Five vertebrae cracked. His back was as taut as a trampoline and he kind of wished someone would jump on it. He stretched and rubbed his eyes. "Are we there?"
"Just about."
"What time is it?"
"Six-thirty."
"Wow, I slept that long?"
"Yep, Chilcolten turnoff is just ahead."
Michael straightened up. The highway was divided with a weedy patch of grass separating the west and east lanes. A logging truck, loaded with bouncing fir trees, roared fifty feet ahead of them. A pair of Harley Davidsons rumbled from behind. Michael's stomach growled. He looked into a blue Sienna, in the fast lane on their left. The dad was driving, and the mom and two kids, a boy and a girl about ten, were staring at Chris and Michael like they were aliens. Michael leaned over Chris and stuck out his tongue. They turned away.

A river twisted through a huge sand bank in a gully about eighty feet below on Michael's right. It was tough to see with the trees whizzing by. To his left the mountains rose beyond his view. Massive fir trees engulfed them. How could Katherine survive up there?

The sky was powder blue, and the wispy clouds made it look cold.

He shivered and pushed the air vent towards the door.

Michael turned to the back of the truck. Thomas's head stretched over the back seat and bounced like he had no spine. His mouth gaped open and he breathed in wisps. How could I live with myself if Katherine died? Michael thought. I'd never be able to look at Thomas again, or Dad, or Jane, or Greg, or anyone for that matter.

Grief rose from his gut like bile and he felt like a monster, a lonely, useless one. What was really the point in living anyway? How many kids had he beaten the crap out of? They'd be happy to see him dead. His eyes burned. He turned to the dash and hid his face with his hand. He hated crying. Crying was for wimps.

I'll jump off a cliff, that's what. If Katherine dies, then I die.

Michael rubbed the tears with the palm of his hand and sat up straight in his seat. "Is this highway one?"

"Yep," Chris said. "Which exit?"

"I'll tell you."

The mountains pulled away to a grass plain that stretched farther than Michael could see. They drove under a set of power lines, held two hundred feet in the air by massive skeleton-like towers that reminded him of the Gates of Argonath in the Lord of the Rings. The sky grew hazy ahead, and Michael guessed Chilcolten was smothered under it somewhere.

"Thirteen kilometers," Chris said.

Michael glanced at the speed sign and grinned. It was the size of a building. "You sure?"

They whipped by a red shack on the right side of the highway. "Wonder what that's for." Michael asked.

"What?"

"The little red building you just drove by."

"Dunno."

Chris squirmed. "There's an intersection coming up, Michael. Do I take it?"

"Not this one," Michael said. "Next one. Valdor Road."

At the Valdor Road exit, Chris merged the truck to the right and off the highway.

"Turn left at the lights," Michael said.

Chris swung to the left lane and accelerated up the ramp.

"Slow down," Michael said. "Photo-radar."

Chris blew through the green light and careened onto Valdor. It was a four-lane road and the traffic was thick. He pulled in behind a rusty Dodge truck and slowed to a crawl.

"Where do I turn?"

"Just before the bridge. Left at Chilcolten Lake Road. Pull into Burger King first. I'm hungry."

CHAPTER 25

The bathroom had always been Katherine's favorite hideout. She could lock the door, it was dark and quiet, the bubble bath soap smelled like strawberries, and the tile floor was cool against her cheek. She'd lay there for hours. It was safe.

But this tile wasn't smooth. It was sharp like broken glass. The strawberries smelled like dirt. And light glowed through her eyelids. She breathed deep, pulling in a cloud of dust, and sneezed. She opened her eyes.

She wasn't lying down. She was perched on a cliff. The tile was rock and the smells were moss. She looked up and gasped. She was eighty feet from the top. How did she get down? She couldn't remember, it was as though her body had climbed without her.

She stretched out her right leg, felt a ledge with her toes, and put her weight on it. The ledge crumbled. Her fingers slipped, and she fell. Her bum hit the ground and a sharp pain reverberated up her spine and through every bone and muscle in her body. She stiffened and took shallow breaths until the pain subsided. She flexed her arms and legs, looked up, and giggled. "Just a five-foot fall. Hilarious."

She pushed herself off the ground, dusted her clothes, picked up the water bottle and pressed it to her lips. The warm water soothed her throat. She tied the water bottle into the shirt, picked it up, and walked along the ledge to the boulder she had stepped off of three hours ago. A shadow covered the east side of the valley. Night fell quickly up here.

She stepped onto the first boulder, slid, and broke into a run. She gasped. She jumped off the boulder, landed on a second one, skidded half way down it and sat on her bum. "Goodness."

She stood up and placed her right foot forward. It slid and she had to step forward to avoid the splits. The pitch propelled her and she broke into a jog, and then a near run. She reached the boulder's edge and leapt for the next one. Landing just after the edge she slid a couple of feet and helicoptered her arms, almost falling back into a crevice. Her heart pounded in fear. She shortened her steps, which slowed her, but her arms swung wildly to keep her in control. She leapt to the next bolder, hopped, slid down it, and leapt to the next one.

Katherine was half way down the rockslide and, though balanced between fear and panic, she was happy with how fast she'd made it. She wondered when the boys would arrive and how they'd find her without a phone. She'd light a big fire when she got to the plane. But if the bad guys knew where the plane had crashed they might find her first. She remembered her bike and felt angry. She'd fixed that bike herself and it was abandoned in a ditch, bent and broken. Those jerks had messed up everything.

She hopped onto the last rock and shortened her steps, trying to stop, but couldn't. She slid down and just before falling off the boulder leapt, hung suspended, and hit the scree. A mini-avalanche of shale carried her and as it slowed she leapt again, landed, and rode another avalanche for eight feet.

Yay, she thought. Dangerous but fast and fun. If she fell she'd tumble five hundred feet, but if she jumped at the right spot, she'd ride waves of shale in a controlled chaos. This was like skiing combined with Hulk-like hopping. She had only skied a couple of times in her life on school field trips. It had been too expensive of a sport and she'd never have asked her mom to spend the money.

Katherine stepped from the shale and onto solid ground. It had taken her thirty minutes to traverse the avalanche. She sat down under the shade of a tree and panted. The terrain was steep, but the trees were sparse and the ground was barren. She stood up and ran to a tree, grabbed it to slow her ascent, and then ran to the next one. She'd reach the valley in no time at this rate.

CHAPTER 26

Chris shoved the last piece of burger into his mouth, wiped his face with his arm, and turned on the left signal light while slowing the truck. Michael grinned. Six months ago Chris couldn't steer and turn on the radio at the same time.

Thomas rustled in the back seat. "Are we there?" he asked.

Michael turned back to him.

The seat pattern was engraved in Thomas's face. He rubbed his eyes.

"Almost, just gotta turn here. You slept a long time." Michael grabbed the bag at his feet and tossed it on Thomas's lap. "Have a burger."

"How long till we get there?" Thomas asked.

"About an hour's drive. Then we hike."

Chris accelerated onto Chilcolten Lake Road, a dual lane, paved road with double yellow lines down the center, a concrete block barrier on the right side, and a steep hill on the left. The shoulder weeds were stunted and yellow. The Chilcolten River ran to their right, about forty feet down a steep gully. One hundred feet across, it snaked through huge gravel beds. The water glittered in the setting sun and danced over rocks, polished and colored like eggs in an Easter basket.

Power lines sagged between weathered poles set along the side of the road. The place looked tired, but comforting and pretty. Michael grinned. *Pretty, a Katherine word.*

They drove in silence passing a mobile trailer park, a paint ball field, and a bed and breakfast. Michael's eyelids drooped and he slumped in his seat. He thought back to when he was seven years old. He would stare out the car window then, and let the scenery coax him into a dimension where there was no time. He'd conceive devious ideas there and had designed his hideout, mapped out the camera and speaker system he'd installed in their home, and planned his attacks on Chris.

He hoped Katherine would be easy to find. It would be dark and hard to keep their bearings in the forest. Hopefully, the plane had crashed close to the trail. But what if she was hurt, or was stuck on a mountain? They might have to strap a stretcher together and carry her out, if they ever found her.

A sliver of sun rested on top of the mountain range. It turned brilliant, as though it was throwing a final show before vanishing to the other side of the world. The trees were taller and hugged the road, bordering it like an army of soldiers. Michael glanced above into the cut-line of sky. In spite of the sun's remnants a few stars were visible from millions of light years away.

The sun dropped. Night fell like a blanket, turning the road into a tunnel. Michael shuddered. It felt like a trap. The trees turned black and menacing. Katherine must be scared to death out there, he thought.

The yellow lines shimmered in the headlights and animal eyes glinted back from the trees. "This could be a great start to a horror movie," Michael said.

"Shoot," Chris said.

"What?"

Chris glanced into the rear view mirror. "Headlights behind us, coming up fast."

Michael looked back into a pair of blue-white lights. The driver turned on the high beams and the brilliant light burned Michael's retinas, creating green spots in his vision.

Chris flipped down the rear view mirror. "I don't like this."

The vehicle was a truck, or a large SUV. It accelerated towards them. Michael gripped his seat.

"He's gonna hit us!" Thomas yelled.

The headlights disappeared under their tailgate and the vehicle slammed into them. Their truck lurched and Michael's head snapped forward. Chris swung the steering wheel left and right, fighting the truck as it slid sideways. "Hold on!" Chris yelled.

Their truck flipped over, flew through the air and slammed onto its hood. The windshield burst into a cloud and a million diamond-like pieces of glass showered the cab. The roof caved onto Michael's head and he ducked into his seat. Pain bolted through his neck and black dots swarmed like locusts in his vision. He smelled gasoline. Thomas screamed. The truck rolled onto its tires and bounced into a wall of trees. Michael threw up his arm. The air bag blew with the sound of a gunshot and slammed his arm into his face. Branches snapped and gored the truck's side, shrieking like terrified children. They careened down the gully, snapping trees like chop sticks, and hit the river. Water smacked Michael's face. He fell into black.

CHAPTER 27

Katherine tripped over a root, or a rock, and fell into a tree. The bark scraped the scabs off her arm and she bit her lip to hold back the scream. She cursed for not bringing the flashlight.

She had been stumbling in the dark for what seemed like an hour.

She rose to her feet and crept forward, looking for a place to sleep. A huge shadow appeared. More than double her height, and round, it looked like the cutting head of a tunnel-boring machine she'd once seen on the news. She crept up to it. A tree had fallen, creating a round wall of dirt from its base, which was infused with roots that looked like giant worms. She trekked around the roots, placed her hand on the tree trunk, and marched along it. She found a depression underneath. She dropped to her hands and knees and crawled in. It was big enough for two people, lined with soft moss, and had one opening. She snuggled into the moss and smiled.

Something fell onto her head, dug into her hair, and buzzed like a fly caught in a web. She screeched. It worked through her tendrils of hair and latched onto her skull with hooked claws. She wrapped her hand around it and worked it from her hair. It poked at her fingers, flapped its wings, and tried to dig its way out. It had to be a beetle, a big one. She crawled out and threw it to the ground. The leaves rustled as it scuttled away.

She knelt and felt her way around the forest floor, looking for dry sticks, pine cones and moss.

The sunset illuminated the snow-capped peaks with a brilliant and fluorescent pink. It was the most beautiful thing she'd ever seen. But like heaven and hell, the valley was the opposite, black and menacing.

She untied the shirt, spread it on the ground, and felt around it for the matches and moss. She placed the moss on the ground in front of her and struck a match to it. A two inch flame licked up and she added some twigs and branches. The flames grew to her knees and she tossed on more wood until they reached her waist. The fire bathed her hideout in light, and in spite of the mottled tree above and the thousands of bugs it held, it looked comfortable. *Goodness, the fire felt good.*

After her arms and legs had warmed, she went into the forest and gathered dry wood, and stacked it into a pile up to her knees,

A lone wolf howled.

She tore a strip off of her shirt and pushed it into the gun barrel, and shoved it to the end with a stick. She pulled it out. It was wet. Tearing off more strips she pushed them in and out until they remained dry. She loaded the gun and armed it. "Hope it's not plugged."

She threw some wood onto the fire, crawled into the hole, crossed her legs, and rocked. Her heartbeat synchronized with the dancing flames. Her eyelids grew heavy. The gun fell from her hands. She passed into a deep sleep.

CHAPTER 28

White lights swirled through Michael's head. He could hear Thomas calling him from somewhere in the distance. His legs felt like frozen popsicles. Pain radiated from his nose, up through his temples, and around the back of his head.

"Michael! Wake up!" Michael felt someone's weight on his chest. His seat belt clicked and someone grabbed his shoulders and pulled him towards the door. He pushed the hands away. "Hold on. Wait. What's going on?" He opened his eyes. The river sparkled under the moon's glow. White powder covered the truck's dash, and the airbag was splayed out like a broken eggshell and splattered with blood. He turned to Thomas. "What? Where are we?"

"We crashed. We're in the river." Michael glanced at the driver's seat. "Where's Chris? Is he okay?"

"I think his arm is broken," Thomas said. "He's in the back, looking for the backpack. Come on. There's gasoline everywhere. You've gotta get out."

"Are you okay?" Michael asked.

"Not a scratch," Thomas said.

"Is my nose broken?"

"I think your face is broken. Come on. Let's splash some water on you."

Michael placed his feet onto the running board and slid into the river. The water flowed up over his knees. He leaned onto Thomas's shoulder and stood up. The trees spun around him and his knees collapsed. Thomas grabbed him under the arms and pinned him to the truck. "You okay?"

"Yeah, I think so. Just dizzy, for a sec. I'm good now."

Michael stepped around the truck door. It was crushed and disfigured, like a contemporary sculpture. He knelt to the river. A purple and green sheen of gasoline swirled over the surface. He walked further in until the sheen was gone, and cupped water in his hands. He splashed it onto his face. Blood streamed down his hands and arms. He turned and looked at Thomas. "Better?"

Thomas grimaced. "Better toss some more on."

Michael knelt down and plunged his head under the water. It was freezing and felt great. He rubbed his face and hair and pulled his head out, gasping for air. He stood up and staggered to the shore and leaned on the truck. He ran his fingers through his hair, and found an egg-sized lump on top of his head. He shuffled to the tailgate. Chris's feet were sticking out from under the bed cover. A backpack slid out and fell to the ground. Chris wiggled out, hopped down, and looked at Michael. His mouth dropped. "You okay?"

"Feels like someone's beating my head with a rubber mallet. But I'm fine. Why do you guys keep asking me that?"

"You have black eyes and I think your nose is crooked."

"'Splains it," Michael said. "And your arm?"

"Hurts like hell."

"Let's have a look."

Chris rolled his left forearm over. A purple bump protruded from it.

Michael grabbed the backpack, unzipped the front pocket, and pulled out a first aid kit. "Sling or splint?"

"Splint. I can't punch with a sling," Chris said. "And I'm gonna punch his lights out when I find the driver of that truck."

Michael pulled out a roll of gauze. "Thomas, find me a stick, big enough to support Chris's arm. Chris, hold your breath, or something."

Michael wrapped the gauze down Chris's forearm and over the bump, watching Chris grimace with each rotation. Thomas handed Michael a stick, green and about a half-inch thick.

Michael held it up. "Perfect. Thanks, Thomas."

He placed the stick on the inside of Chris's forearm and wrapped it with gauze until secure. He grabbed a role of fluorescent pink tape and bound Chris's forearm in it. "Looks like a girly popsicle. Let me know if your hand turns blue." He placed the first aid kit into the backpack, zipped it up, and gave it to Thomas. "Here, you take it. Come on, let's go."

"Go where?" Thomas asked. How do we get to Katherine now?"

"That inflatable boat would have worked well, eh, Michael?" Chris said.

Michael glared at him. "Shut up, Chris. Come on, let's find us a truck."

The road was thirty feet above them. The hill was steep, and the truck had left a swath of broken trees that looked impassable.

"I'll never get up there," Chris said.

"Over here," Thomas called.

"Where are you?" Michael asked.

"About thirty steps downstream."

"Come on, Chris." Michael limped down the shore. It was covered with wet shale and he slipped and stumbled. He found Thomas staring up the hill. It was still steep. The birch trees glowed like bleached skeletons under the moon's light. The trees were sparse and the ground clear.

"Can you do it?" Michael asked.

"I'll try," Chris said."

"I'll try first," Michael said. He breathed deep, leapt over the rocks, and dashed towards the hill. His foot sunk into a mud patch and stuck, and he fell onto his chest. His head exploded into fireworks. "Gah! That hurt."

"You all right?" Thomas asked.

"Think so." Michael stood up and pulled his foot out of the mud. He stared at a tree, about twelve feet up. He sprung forward, ran up the hill, scrambled to the tree, grabbed it, and pulled himself up. "Come on, Chris, give it a shot."

Chris stepped around the mud and looked at Michael. His eyes were wide and white. He hunched down and sprinted up the hill. He tripped over a rock, slid back, and fell onto his broken arm. "Aagghhhh! Crap! That hurt." Tears glinted in his eyes. He pushed himself into a three-point stance and powered up the slope like a three-legged bulldog. He grabbed the tree trunk, wrapped his right arm around it, and whimpered.

"One more," Michael said. "Come on." He scrambled to the next tree, pushed himself off it, and crawled on his knees to the road.

"Come on, Chris."

Chris dashed up past the tree and fell. He started to slide backwards. Michael lay on his stomach and grabbed Chris's right arm. Thomas appeared below and pushed his shoulder into Chris's bum. They dragged Chris up. He crawled onto the road and lay on his stomach, whimpering.

"You okay, Chris?" Michael asked.

"Think so."

"Come on." Michael stood up, grabbed Chris under his arm and pulled him to his feet.

"Did you guys see the truck that ran us off the road?" Chris asked.

Thomas stood. "No. You think it was Bill and Brandon?"

"Who else?" Michael asked.

"Where are we going?" Thomas asked.

"There's a house a few hundred feet back. A brand new Ford Raptor's in the driveway."

"How do you know?" Chris asked.

The trees started to spin. Michael squared his shoulders and stared at the ground, mapping out each step. His cheeks and nose throbbed. He clenched his teeth and pain streaked through his jaw and into his temples. Stars flooded his eyes. He pushed his right foot out, and then his left. "We drove by it. Come on."

"Do you think they've reached Katherine?" Thomas asked.

Michael bit his lip, and stared at the ground. He stopped and looked at Thomas. "I wish I could say no, but they're probably close to the crash site by now."

"We better hurry," Thomas said. He pushed by Michael and sprinted down the road. Michael ran after him. Stars fired through his eyes with every step.

They came to a rusty mailbox mounted on top of a wood post beside a dirt driveway. Michael crouched and peered down the driveway to a small bungalow with two bedroom windows on the right and a large, picture window on the left. The bedrooms were dark, but the living room lights were on and a television flashed patterns onto a faded curtain. A black Ford Raptor sat in the driveway, parked in front of a single garage attached to the house.

"How the heck did you see that?" Thomas asked.

"I see everything," Michael said. He grinned. "Stay low."

"We're stealing it?" Thomas asked.

"Yep."

"But, we can't."

"Do you wanna get your sister or not?"

Michael crept down the dirt road and dashed alongside the truck to the passenger door. A light, mounted on the garage, turned on and flooded the yard, driveway, and surrounding trees with dazzling, white light. "Get down!" Michael said. Chris and Thomas dropped beside him, and they cowered behind the front wheel. The front door screeched open. A man ducked under the doorframe and stepped onto the balcony. Michael could see his biceps flex from fifty feet away. The man glanced around the yard and walked back into the house, slamming the door behind him.

"Backpack, Thomas."

Thomas pulled off the pack and passed it to Michael. Michael zipped it open and felt around for a smooth object.

"What are you looking for?" Chris whispered.

"A gadget. I made it over the summer."

"What does it do?"

"Just watch." Michael felt the plastic in his hand and pulled it out.

"An apple TV?" Chris asked.

"I used the shell," Michael said. He felt for a small switch on the side and pushed it on. He pulled his phone from his pocket and connected a cable on the gadget into his phone. He scanned the phone menu and selected an app. "It'll take a few seconds," he said.

"Where'd you get the app?" Thomas asked.

"It's mine," Michael said.

"You wrote it?" Thomas asked.

"Yep."

The phone beeped. Michael swiped the screen and a green display appeared. He selected the truck make and model, and then pressed an unlock button. The truck door locks clicked. He turned to Chris and grinned. "You wanna drive? Get in."

Michael opened the passenger door and pulled the seat down. Thomas crawled into the back. Michael pushed the seat upright and Chris crawled over the center console into the driver's seat. Michael crawled in and pulled the door closed without slamming it.

"Now what?" Chris whispered.

"As soon as it starts, put it into reverse and back out. And don't take your time. Can you do it with your arm?"

Chris pulled on his seatbelt and grabbed the stick shift. "Watch me."

Michael snapped in his seatbelt and waited until Thomas's clicked. "Okay." He placed his finger on the phone display and slid over a start button. The truck roared to life. "Go!"

Chris placed the truck into reverse and crept down the driveway. The front door of the house banged open and the man ran out, with a shotgun. "Jeez! Hurry!" Michael yelled.

Chris gunned the truck and screeched onto the road. The man was three quarters down the driveway, waving the gun in the air and yelling.

Chris's hand slipped off the gearshift.

"Hurry!" Michael yelled. He could see the man's eyes.

Chris slammed the truck into drive and surged ahead.

"Holy," Michael said. "I never expected that."

"He was mad," Thomas said. "Do you think he'll come after us?"

Chris pressed the accelerator. "Probably, if he has another truck."

"How'd you do that?" Thomas asked.

"I'm getting good, aren't I?" Chris said.

"No, not your driving, Chris. Michael, how'd you start the truck?"

"I patched into Sync."

"What's Sync?"

"It connects the truck to an operator who can remotely stop, unlock, or track it. I added in a start command."

"Can they use it to track us?"

"Only because I'm letting them," Michael said. "That's the genius part. It'll bring the cops right to us. They should get there about the time we're getting Katherine out."

Chris's jaw hardened. "Do you think Bill and Brandon know Katherine's alive?"

"They do now," Michael said. "Why else would we be here?"

Chris frowned. "Good point."

"We gotta get there," Thomas said.

"I'm going as fast as I can," Chris said.

"I'll text her," Thomas said. "I'll tell her to hide."

"If they can use Sync to track us, can they use it to stop the truck?" Chris asked.

"No worries," Michael said, "I've overridden them."

The trees grew thin and the river disappeared. They blew by a right turn into the Chilcolten Lake Provincial Park onto a gravel road and continued around a left bend. The lake opened in front of them. Mountains towered around it, almost impossibly steep. The headlights swept over the surface as Chris headed left, illuminating white capped waves. A massive boulder appeared in the middle of a dirt road, and Chris slowed.

"Time?" Michael said.

Chris glanced at the dash. "Eight thirty."

Michael sat up straight. "Keep going. This road circles the left side of the lake. If I've got her pinned right, Katherine is only about eight miles from where it ends."

Chris veered around the boulder and gunned down the road. It was a cart trail; the ruts and boulders tossed the truck around like a teddy bear in a pillow fight.

"What'll we do when we find Katherine?" Thomas asked.

Chris glanced back. "Good question. What should we do? Mom and Dad won't be back for a few days and Robert... "

"Joe," Thomas said.

Michael glanced back at Thomas. "Geoff."

Chris swung the truck to the right. "Uh, yeah...Geoff, I guess. Let's call him Robert. That's his real name anyway."

The truck's right tire fell into a rut and Michael dropped into his door. The handle dug into his thigh. It felt like lying on a baseball bat. He grimaced and grabbed the hold handle as Chris gunned the engine and vaulted the truck out.

"Where was I?" Chris asked.

"Parents won't be back," Michael said.

"Whew. Yeah, that's right. Our parents won't be back for a few days and Robert's watching the house, I bet."

"Let's just worry about Katherine," Michael said. "She might need a doctor. We'll have to get her to a hospital."

"Sounds like a plan," Chris said. "Thomas?"

"Yep. Get Katherine. What's not to like about that?"

Chris stopped at a gap between the trees. He leaned over Michael and looked at the lake. In the fleeting moonlight Michael could barely make out the opposite shore. "Bigger than I expected."

Chris steered the truck into a sharp left, drove a few hundred feet, and then a right and another right, and a left – driving a square U about six hundred feet across.

"I think we're almost there," Chris said.

Michael looked out the window. "Yep, there's the end of the lake. It empties into the river, or the river empties into it. I never checked that."

Thomas pointed between them. "What's that?"

A large object loomed at the road's end.

Chris crept forward until the object was discernible and clicked on the high beams. The blood red body of a Lincoln Escalade glittered in the headlights.

Chris pulled up beside the Escalade, placed the truck into park and hopped out. He grabbed a flashlight from the backpack and ran it over the vehicle. He crept around the front of the truck and disappeared.

Michael grabbed his phone and stopped the engine. He opened his door and stepped out. The ground was hard. He pulled back the seat and Thomas hopped out beside him.

Chris crept around from behind the truck. "There's no one in it," he said. "The hood is banged up good. Did she answer your text?"

Thomas pulled out his phone. The screen lit up, casting a pale light over his face. He looked like a green ghost. He frowned. "No."

Thomas turned to the trail at the end of the road. "I gotta get her."

"Hold on, Thomas," Michael said. "We need a plan."

Thomas sprinted into the forest.

Michael reached into the truck, grabbed the backpack, and ran after him. "What the...? Chris, help. Thomas, hold on!" Every step thundered into his brain. He staggered and tripped, and sprinted on.

Chris blew by Michael with the only flashlight. It swirled like a light bug and vanished into the trees.

CHAPTER 29

Chris and Thomas sloshed somewhere ahead. Michael stumbled down a slope and splashed into a bog. The water reached his knees and he fell face first. He pushed himself up and wiped the water from his eyes. He ran through the bog. The water became shallow, and he broke onto a dry path, up a hill and under a blanket of fir trees. The forest canopy swallowed the moonlight, and the trail turned a faint grey. The ground dropped and he was propelled forward almost falling before it rose again; he stumbled and dropped to his knees. He jumped up and bolted. The water squished in his runners.

A stitch tore through Michael's side and he clenched his fist. He slipped on a rock, tripped over a root, and flew like an elephant in a pole-vault. Branches whipped his face. He hit the ground and rolled onto his back. Blood trickled over his eyebrow and his ankle stung with pain. He scrambled up and limped on. "Goh! Chris, Thomas, slow down!"

"I've got him!" Chris yelled from ahead. Michael slowed, jogged about fifty feet, and limped through a berry patch. He found Thomas and Chris on the other side, hands on their knees, and panting.

Michael skidded to a stop and collapsed to the ground. "Let's…let's rest. How long, have we been running?"

"Almost forty minutes," Chris said.

Michael sat up and grimaced at the pain in his foot. "Geez, you guys are trying to kill me."

"How can we find her?" Thomas asked.

Michael stood up. "Still hasn't answered the text?"

Thomas shook his head. "No. Should we call out for her?"
"No," Chris said, "she might be hiding."

CHAPTER 30

The sound of snapping branches pierced Katherine's sleep and she woke with a start.

She clenched her teeth and pushed herself to a sitting position. Her stomach felt like a blowtorch was being held to it.

A branch cracked, and then another one. She squinted but could see nothing. "Hello?"

She heard footsteps.

"Katherine?" It was a man's voice. It wasn't Greg or Geoff. "The gun," she whispered. She scanned the ground, but she couldn't see it.

"Hello, Katherine?" The man called louder.

"Ye...yes."

A light broke through the trees. A man walked from the forest, holding a flashlight. He approached her and stood above her. "You okay?" His voice was soothing, but she broke into goose flesh.

"Not really, uh, I think so," she said. "Who, who are you?"

"Name's Brandon." He smiled. "And you must be Katherine."

"How do you know? Who are you?"

Brandon pulled out a radio and clicked the mike. "Bill, I found a treat back here."

"What?"

"The girl."

"Shut up. She is alive then."

"Uh-huh."

"Freakin' unbelievable. She's the only one. You know what to do."

The man put the walkie-talkie into his back pocket and fumbled with something on his hip. Katherine's heart raced. She ran her hands over the ground around her, feeling for the gun.

"Sorry, Katherine," Brandon said.

She heard a snap pop.

"You've lived through a lot, by the looks of you." He leant down in front of her and stroked her hair. He held his other hand behind his back.

She felt a wave of nausea, and pulled her head away. "Don't touch me!"

"Whoa, you're a feisty one!" He laughed, stood up and walked a few steps back.

Katherine's hand brushed metal. She grabbed the gun and held it behind her back.

He drew a pistol and pointed it at her head. Katherine raised the gun and pointed it at his chest. His eyes grew wide and he dropped his smile.

She'd been through too much to let this jerk end it now.

CHAPTER 31

A gunshot blew through the trees and echoed through the valley. Michael's skin erupted into gooseflesh.

Thomas jumped up. "What the heck?"

A second shot cracked.

Thomas's face turned white.

Michael leaned over and puked up his hamburger. Bile ran through his nose and he sneezed. "Crud," he said.

"My sister," Thomas said. "Oh my God, they killed her."

Chris jumped to his feet. "No, Thomas, I can't believe that. Come on. Michael, you take the rear, protect Thomas."

"But... "

"Shut up, Michael! You protect Thomas! And no one talks!"

Chris ducked down and ran towards the gunshot. Thomas followed and disappeared. Michael dashed after him, following the snapping branches. He started to shake. They couldn't save Katherine from a bullet, not out here. He wanted to drop to the ground and decompose into the forest floor. They ran a few hundred feet, stopped, and ducked under a fern.

Chris crouched to the ground. "Can you smell that?"

"What?" Thomas asked.

"Campfire smoke."

"Brandon? Where are you?" A man yelled from somewhere.

"He's on our left," Chris said.

"What now?" Thomas whispered.

Chris put his face right in front of Michael and Thomas. "Look, we can't take on Brandon and Bill, not if they have guns, but we have to find Katherine."

"But she's dead," Thomas said. Tears streamed down his cheeks.

"We don't know that," Chris said. "Come on. Follow me. We'll sneak past them and double back."

Chris hopped over a fallen tree and disappeared.

Michael pushed Thomas. "Go!" Thomas crawled over the tree. He was blubbering. Michael felt dead inside.

Everything looked the same — trees, bushes, roots, and moss. Michael wondered how Chris knew where he was going. He stumbled over a rock and dashed around a tree. "Oof!" He ran into Thomas. "What are you guys... "

"Shush!" Chris said.

Michael heard footsteps running towards them.

Chris dropped to the ground. "Get down!"

The footsteps were soft. Branches weren't snapping under them. And the person was sobbing. And it was a girl.

Thomas jumped up. "Katherine!"

"Katherine?" Chris whispered.

A shadow careened around a tree and stopped in its tracks. Chris turned on the flashlight. Michael gasped. Katherine's face was bloated and red. Her lips were cracked. She had a bald patch on her head. She wore a white, long sleeve shirt stained with blood and her jeans were shredded and bloody. She looked wild, like a hunted animal. Michael stepped back.

"How?" Michael said. He fell to his knees. "Oh thank you, God."

Thomas and Chris ran to Katherine and threw their arms around her. Michael jumped up, ran over, and bear hugged them.

"Ouch, ouch," she said. "Don't touch me, and hurry." Her voice was hoarse. She smelled like gunpowder. "Someone's chasing me. He's got a gun."

"But...but who shot who?" Thomas asked.

Katherine flashed her teeth, and for a second she looked like a demon. "I did. I think I killed him."

"Killed who?"

"Guys!" Katherine said. "Later! Get moving. I dropped my gun."

"Follow me," Chris whispered. "He'll expect us to take the trail. Let's cross it and head west."

"I can hear you!" Bill's yell echoed through the trees. "You're dead! Every one of you."

"Run," Chris whispered. He turned and disappeared into the black of the forest. Hunched like Quasimodo, Katherine hobbled after him. Thomas dashed after her and then Michael. A branch whipped across Michael's face and stung like fire. He yelped and rubbed his face as the ground dropped under him. He tripped down a hill and fell onto his hands and knees at the bottom. "Drat!"

He leapt up and ascended the other side of the gulley. Branches creaked and snapped and Michael followed the noises. *Bill's gonna follow them as well!*

The trees thinned at the top. He skirted through them, jumped over a boulder and stopped. Chris, Katherine, and Thomas were standing in line, staring up a sheer rock face.

"Crap," Thomas said. "Now what?"

Chris pointed towards the cliff base to his left. "Look."

"What?" Thomas asked.

"A cave, or something."

Michael trudged along the cliff towards a dark spot, about thirty feet to their left. He stopped in front of it. Chris, Katherine, and Thomas stepped up beside him.

"An old mine?" Michael asked.

A branch cracked from the forest behind them.

"Don't know," Chris said, "and I don't care. Let's go."

Michael's head pounded. "It gives me the creeps."

Chris dashed to the tunnel and ducked in. Katherine, Thomas, and Michael followed. Chris's light illuminated ugly faces in the tunnel walls.

Chris broke into a jog. "Let's go!"

"I don't know," Michael said.

Katherine and Thomas dashed after him. Michael placed his fingertips on the tunnel wall and shuffled along it. He couldn't see the floor so he followed Chris's light and used the wall to keep his balance. The rock seemed moist and warm, as though it was alive. Michael could swear it was breathing. He started to shake.

He tripped and fell onto his right knee, cracking it into the stone floor. He bit his lip in pain.

Chris slowed to a fast walk. Michael limped behind them. They continued for a few hundred feet. "Hold on," Michael said.

"What?" Chris asked.

Michael placed his back against the cave wall and slid to the floor. "Just stop. Lay low. See if we can hear him."

Chris, Katherine, and Thomas sat beside him. Chris turned off the light. The tunnel became dead quiet. A warm breeze brushed by with a low howl, coming from deep within the cave. "Ssshhh," Michael said. He slowed his breathing.

"I can hear his footsteps," Katherine said.

Chris turned on his flashlight and jumped up. "Let's go." He ran, and Katherine and Thomas followed. Michael groaned and pulled himself off the ground and stumbled after Chris's light, brushing his right hand over the tunnel wall. His knee hurt more than his face.

Chris stopped. "Hey! A fork." His whisper echoed back and down behind them.

Michael skidded to a stop. "Hold on guys." He panted.

Chris turned to him. "What?"

"I've been here before."

Katherine looked to him. She was hunched over, panting, and looked brittle. Michael wondered if she'd make it. "What?" she asked.

"Follow me," Michael said. He picked up the backpack and pulled out a glow stick and a white device, about the size and shape of an egg, with a black speaker in its side. "We need to go left. Bill has to go right. Bunch up close together and follow me. Chris, I need to borrow your flashlight." Michael grabbed the flashlight, placed his right hand on the cave wall and walked into the tunnel. Thomas appeared to his left. Katherine and Chris shuffled along behind them.

"You said left," Thomas said.

"I know," Michael said. "Trust me." They crept down the tunnel and around a curve. A wooden bridge appeared. It was made with rough-hewn beams, eight inches square, and decked with half-inch wood planks. Seven feet long, it spanned a circular hole that looked like a giant water well. Michael dropped to his knees and peered over the edge. A throaty growl emanated from deep below. A warm breeze rose up and tussled his hair. Michael shined the flashlight down, but the beam was swallowed up by the darkness. He stood, cracked the glow stick, and threw it over the bridge to the other side. It cast a green glow.

"What's that for?" Chris asked.

"That tells Bill we went over the bridge," Michael said. He pulled the gadget from his pocket and turned it on. "This thing creates a low frequency sound. It's barely audible, but will make this side of the tunnel more inviting. Michael placed the speaker on the ground. "Chris, pass me a jacket or something from the backpack."

"Sleeping bag?"

"Perfect."

Chris unlatched the backpack, pulled out a sleeping bag, and passed it to Michael. He unfurled it and gave Chris the flashlight. "Okay, stay together and walk out the way we came in. Michael placed his hand on Chris's back and swept the sleeping bag over the ground behind him, dusting over their footprints. They exited the tunnel at the fork. Bill's footsteps were louder. He was walking a quick pace.

"Hurry," Michael said. "I'll lead and point the flashlight back. We need to walk on the same spot, so there's only one set of footsteps. Michael took the flashlight from Chris and walked into the left tunnel.

"But he'll see the footsteps," Chris said.

"I know," Michael said. "He'll think we're trying to fool him into going this way."

"Seriously?" Chris said. "We're going this way so he'll think we went the other way?"

"Stranger than fiction," Michael said. The tunnel curved to the left. Michael crept on until they rounded the curve, and then he counted fifty steps. He stopped, leaned his back onto the wall, and sat down. Chris, Katherine, and Thomas sat beside him. Michael turned off the light. "Ssshhh."

Bill's footsteps grew louder. He was panting. He stopped. Michael envisioned him staring at the two paths, wondering which way to go.

Bill started to walk. His footsteps echoed down the tunnel, and grew louder.

Now I've done it, Michael thought.

Bill continued, closer and closer. Michael could see his flashlight glittering off the tunnel walls.

"Little brats. I'll kill 'em." The light disappeared and the footsteps receded. Michael sighed.

Bill's footsteps slowed and stopped. Michael counted to sixty. A loud crack echoed through the cave. "No!" Bill yelled. "Help!" He screamed.

"Bridge went," Michael said. He stood and turned on the

flashlight. "We're safe now."

"Did he...fall?" Katherine asked.

"Afraid so," Michael said. "It was him or us."

Michael leaned his arm onto the cave wall and his forehead onto his arm. He'd never felt this tired before. A lump formed in his throat.

He felt Katherine's hand on his back. "Michael? How could you have known?"

A green hue enveloped the cave. Katherine spun around. "What?"

"Things are about to get real interesting," Michael said.

A ball of light rose from the floor, about eight feet into the tunnel. It broke into a mist. The mist swirled and formed into a flowing dress. Green eyes shone from above the dress and a woman's face formed around the eyes.

"Hi, Mom," Michael said.

"Mom?" Chris said.

"It was you," Katherine said.

"Hello, Michael. Hello, Chris. Katherine, Thomas – you guys okay?"

"Uh-huh," they answered in unison.

Michael's mom gazed into his eyes. Warmth flooded his heart, his legs, his feet, and his arms. "Michael, I died for you. Wear it with honor, not with shame. You can feel bad for what you've done to others, but don't let that drag you down. It's over now."

"Uh-huh," Michael said.

"Your parents know what's best for you, Michael. You have to promise me, you'll see the counselor."

"But... "

"Are you going to argue with me, Michael? You've got a lot of anger inside and you need help dealing with it. Promise?"

Michael stared at her, unblinking. "Okay, fine."

"Take care of yourself, Michael. You can't help others until you help yourself; and helping others is what you do best. And put that money to good use, and get Katherine, Thomas, and their mom into the clinic as well. They've got some healing of their own to do."

You'll be a great man, Michael. I love you, okay?"

Michael had a lump in his throat and he couldn't talk over it. "Okay," he squeaked. "I love you too, Mom."

"Chris. You're all I could ask for in an elder son. You have a great love for your brother and for all others. Most of all, you're kind. Your confidence is blooming. Your attributes will serve you well. Take care of your brother. You are a leader, Chris; and one day you'll get the chance to show it. Okay?"

"Ye...yes, Mom. I love you."

"I love you too."

"Katherine, Thomas, you're the most loyal of friends and both the bravest people I know. You've suffered greatly and have flourished in spite of it. Thomas, you've got some tough times ahead I'm afraid, but you will accomplish things you didn't know possible."

"And, Michael and Christopher, though I did not bear you, make no mistake -- you have always been my children, and always will be."

"Yes, Mom." Chris said.

I have to go now. I won't be here to protect you but will always look upon you. So be good."

A brilliant light flooded the ceiling. Their mom smiled at them, looked to the light, and rose into it.

The cave collapsed into darkness.

"Whoh," Chris said. "That was cool."

CHAPTER 32

Katherine's head felt like it was full of dough -- hot, bloated, and expanding into her skull. Bolts of pain shot through her eyes, and her ears throbbed. She focused on the sounds. Something beeped in her ear. People were talking in hushed voices and shoes squeaked down linoleum floors. The wobble-wobble of gurney wheels whisked by. It smelled like rubber bands and she wanted to vomit. She lay on her back and a bright light shone against her eyelids, but she had no interest in opening them.

The plane crash flashed through her mind and she breathed deep. She felt the coffin tumble, her stomach flip as she fell from the sky, her wonder as the green bubble formed and saved her, and looking back at her lifeless body. Her legs and arms started to shake and she clenched her fists.

She smelled baby powder. *Ponds cream.*

"Mom?"

She opened her eyes to a fluorescent bulb behind a yellowed diffuser. She moved her legs and gasped as a bolt of pain streaked through them. She drew her eyes down. She was in a hospital bed. Her arms were bound with bandages. Her mom was sitting at her side.

Her mom's eyes widened and her jaw fell open. "Katherine?"

"I think so. Am I alive?"

Her mom smiled. "Yes, very much."

"Can you lift the bed?"

"Sure." Her mom grabbed a remote and touched a button, and

the bed whirred, lifting Katherine to a reclined sitting position. The hospital room walls were eggshell bland, broken only by a picture window to her right. It was dark outside.

Her mom leaned forward and hugged her, and sobbed. Her tears ran down Katherine's cheek.

'I thought I'd lost you," she whispered.

"I'm sorry, Mom."

"Sorry?"

"I didn't mean to get mad."

"Oh, Katherine, don't give it another thought."

"Mom?"

"Yes?"

"Thanks."

"For what?"

"For getting us away, from him."

Her mom drew back, wiped the tears from her face, and tilted her head to the side. "Dad?"

"Yeah."

Her mom glanced down. "I should have done more, Katherine. I should have protected you. I was a coward."

"You did the best you could. Can you stop feeling guilty about it?"

"It'll be hard. I'll try, but only if you don't scare me like that again."

Katherine grinned. "Have you been trying to find me?"

"I've been to Mexico, and back, believe it or not."

"You went on holidays?"

Her mom laughed. "No! Of course not. I'll tell you about it later. Anyway, we got back this morning."

"We?"

"It's complicated. Chris's parents. Really, I'll tell you all later."

"Okay then. What time is it?"

"Nine o'clock. You've been asleep for two days. Though they've got you pretty drugged up. You're a real mess, I'm afraid."

Katherine's gaze followed the needle in her hand, up the clear tube, and to the IV bottle. "I'm a cat, Mom. I have nine lives, or had nine. I've got five now."

Brandon's face flashed through Katherine's mind.

The firelight had reflected the terror in his eyes as her gun had gone off. He'd been staring right into her as though pleading. She'd shot him a second time. His spirit had leapt from his eyes and he'd collapsed to the ground.

"Katherine, are you all right?"

"I...I killed someone, Mom."

"I know, honey. I heard. I'm so sorry. But if you hadn't? Would you be here now?"

Shoes squeaked down the hallway. They grew louder. A nurse walked by and continued down the hall.

Katherine looked back at her mom. "No, I guess not. But I had no idea what it would...feel like. He looked at me, Mom, as he died. I'll never forget that look. I keep seeing him, over and over."

"I can't image how that must feel, sweetheart. But, you had no choice. You know that, right?"

"Yeah, but I'll never forget him. He didn't deserve that."

"How's Thomas?" Katherine asked.

"Good. He thought you had died. I think that changed him."

Katherine pushed onto her elbows, lifting her back off the bed. "Changed him? How?"

"A little solemn. Maybe he'll come back to his old self when he sees you."

"Yeah, he's such a happy little guy. Where is he?"

"Back at the hotel, with everyone else. I told him I'd call when you woke up."

"Are we in Chilcolten?"

"Yes."

Katherine lay back. "Could you not call tonight? I'm too tired." Katherine closed her eyes. Her mom said something, but Katherine spiraled into sleep before she caught it.

Katherine heard Chris whispering, but couldn't catch the words. She opened her eyes to a brilliant sunrise. Chris and Michael were leaning against the window ledge, talking. She looked to her left, to Thomas, sitting on her bed. He jumped, broke into a smile, flopped onto her, and gave her a bear hug. It hurt, but she didn't mind. He sobbed. "I thought you were dead."

She wrapped her arms around his back and squeezed hard. "Are you kidding, Thomas? I'll always be here for you. I sung our song, you know?"

"So did I."

Chris appeared above them. "Hey, chick, how are ya?"

"Hi, Katherine," Michael said. He stayed by the window. His eyes were black and his face was swollen.

Thomas tried to stand up, but Katherine didn't let him go. "You okay?" She whispered in his ear.

"I'm just glad you're here," he said.

She gave him an extra hug and released him. His eyes were flooded with tears, but he glowed like he was looking at a puppy.

"Hey, guys, can I talk to Chris alone?"

Michael and Thomas glanced at each other. "Sure."

Katherine patted the bed beside her and Chris sat down. His arms were stiff by his sides. She sat up and hugged him. "I'm so sorry, Chris." He was shaking. "I didn't mean to get angry with you. I want to be together, always. Okay?"

"Me too."

"Chris?"

He lifted his head and looked at her. "Uh-huh?"

"Did we really see your mother's ghost or was I hallucinating?"

"Either we saw my mother's ghost or we were all hallucinating," he said.

"Did you hear what she said about Thomas?"

Chris frowned. "Yes. I don't know what she meant."

"Neither do I. I'm scared."

"We'll protect him," Chris said. "Don't worry."

"Can you have Michael come in? I'd like to talk to him alone as well."

Chris furrowed his eyebrows. "Uh, sure." He left the room.

Katherine grabbed the remote and raised the incline on her bed.

Michael walked in, and stood by the door.

"Michael?" Katherine said. "You okay?"

Michael looked at her and she gasped. His eyes looked so much like his mom's. He glanced down and then back up at her. "It's good to see you," he said. "I was sure you were dead."

"Yeah, you and everyone else, apparently," she said. "What's wrong, Michael? What do you need to tell me?"

He shifted his weight from side to side. "This was all my fault."

His chin trembled and he glanced around the room as though

looking for an escape. "I wanted Robert to find us. I took his money to make him mad. I thought I could take him down if he went after us."

"Yeah, I figured that," she said. "Michael, come here."

He shuffled up the right side of her bed like his ankles were in chains. Katherine raised her arms and pulled him down to her. She squeezed him hard. He was breathing deep. "I'm so sorry," he said. "The last thing I wanted was for you to get hurt."

"Michael, I forgive you. No more guilt pulling you down, okay? It's time to start over."

"Okay," he sniffled. "Thank you, Katherine. You're a saint."

CHAPTER 33

Michael yawned and stretched. He was in Katherine's hospital room, sitting on the ledge, his back resting against the window. Chris was beside him and Thomas was slumped in a chair beside Katherine's bed. They had been watching her sleep for the past hour. She looked better but terrible with the missing hair and skin. It had been a tough couple of days for her. The nurses had coaxed her out of bed half a dozen times a day and had walked her around the ward. At first she couldn't even stand up. Now, she was able to make the trek, but the tightness in her face when she walked the hallway showed the pain she was in. She was a tough girl.

Their dad peeked around the door, called Chris and Michael over with a nod of his head, and looked at Thomas. "You mind if we leave you alone for a bit?"

"No, that's fine."

Michael stood up and walked to the door. Greg was leaning against the wall across the hallway. His arms were crossed and his jaw clenched. He nodded at Michael and turned to follow their dad. Their dad led them down the ward floor and onto the elevator; Greg pressed the lobby button. The elevator hummed but didn't feel like it was moving. Michael looked at his dad and then Greg. They didn't seem mad, at least, but their mouths were tight and they were avoiding Michael's eyes. The elevator doors crawled open and their dad led them down the hall, outside the hospital doors, and to his new truck--a red Avalanche, like the old one. He leaned against the side of it and turned to them.

"What's up?" Michael asked.

"Reality," their dad said. He glanced into the trees surrounding the parking lot and licked his lips. "We've got to tell you what's going on, for your protection."

Michael held his breath. *Finally.*

Greg walked up beside their dad and turned to them. "First, the machine."

Michael's heart pumped hard. A black Lincoln swung into the lot and Greg followed it with his eyes. It pulled into a stall, the driver's door opened, and a cane appeared. An elderly man heaved himself from the car and shuffled towards the hospital.

"Any idea what it is?" Greg asked.

Michael and Chris looked at each other and shrugged.

"I wish you were sitting down," Greg said, "but here you go…it's a time machine."

Michael snickered. His dad glared at him and he stopped.

"Serious?" Chris said.

"Uh-huh," their dad said.

Greg looked around again. "And Robert has it."

"So it was him with the helicopters," Chris said.

"Yes," their dad said.

"What can he do with it?" Michael asked.

"Immediately, nothing," their dad said. "We'd only managed to push a fruit fly a minute ahead. It needs a lot of work and a massive power source if he wants to do something serious with it."

"How long does he need?" Chris asked.

Michael's arms prickled. His heart raced. He had never felt this scared, but he was excited as well. "Time doesn't exist anymore, Chris."

Chris looked at him. "Huh?"

"He's right," Greg said. "Time is broken."

"So, what does that mean?" Chris asked.

"They can send someone from the future back with the technology to finish it," Michael said.

"True," their dad said. "They can speed up the design significantly. But a power source like that would take a good five years to build."

"But," Michael said, "they can go anywhere at any time."

"If they figure out how to take people to a specific location and time. And the software to do that would take decades to develop."

"Or ten seconds from now if they bring it back," Michael said.

Greg glanced at his feet. "Mm-hmm."

They watched a man leave the hospital wearing green hospital garb. He climbed into a BMW parked out front and drove off.

"We're not really sure what it means," their dad said. "But things could get real ugly. We're going to build an underground bunker. Robert's a power hungry man. He could start world war three with this thing."

"You really think we're in that much danger?" Chris asked.

Greg looked into the sky and down at Chris. "Yes," he said.

EPILOGUE

Michael sat on the front steps of their home and stared into the night sky. It was clear and the stars were out by the billions. He shivered and zipped up his coat.

Odd things had happened over the past weeks. Reports of flashing lights and massive gravity and magnetic pole fluctuations filled the news, and most of them around the town of Silvertip. Michael knew exactly what they were. And he knew they were strong enough to bring down a plane.

He smelled ozone. The air crackled and the sky lit up with pink and green waves of northern lights. Northern lights never came this far south. Michael looked at his compass. The needle spun, as he'd expected. "They're here," he whispered. "They're here." He glanced towards the massive hole where the barn once stood. It was forty feet deep and the concrete forms were constructed. They'd start the pour tomorrow. "Good," he said. He got up and walked into the house. Katherine, Thomas, and Chris were in the movie room, fixing up bowls of popcorn.

ABOUT THE AUTHOR

Camping, hiking, fishing, hunting, and getting into trouble. What a great way to grow up. One of my favorite memories is sitting on the handlebars of my brother's bike, my dog on my lap, as he careened down the steep mountain trails above our home in Kamloops, BC. My brother and I had caves, tree forts, frog filled ponds, and cactus patches to play in, and sling shots for protection. Somehow I survived my childhood and proudly moved on to fatherhood. My children, Christopher, Michael, Thomas, and Katherine, kindly donated their names, characters, and ideas to the Boulton Quest series of books.

www.NDRichman.com

Made in the USA
Charleston, SC
21 March 2014